THE
MOQUETTE
MYSTERY

Andrew Martin is the author of the bestselling guide to London Transport moquette patterns, *Seats of London*. Among his many novels are ten thrillers featuring the railway detective Jim Stringer, including *The Necropolis Railway* and *The Somme Stations*. His most recent non-fiction book is the *Sunday Times* Bestseller, *To the Sea by Train*. He also writes the 'Reading on Trains' Substack.

www.martinesque.co.uk

THE McQUETTE MYSTERY

ANDREW MARTIN

SAFE HAVEN

Published 2025 by Safe Haven Books Ltd
12 Chinnocks Wharf
14 Narrow Street
London E14 8DJ
www.safehavenbooks.co.uk

A catalogue record for this book
is available from the British Library.

ISBN 978 1 0685162 4 5

1 3 5 7 9 10 8 6 4 2

Typeset in Perpetua by M Rules Ltd

Printed and bound in the UK by
Clays Ltd, Elcograf, S.p.A.

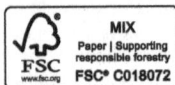

1

Thursday, August 4th, was likely to end up being counted the hottest day of 1938 so far. This according to Ann Jones, the lift girl at Quarmby & Bates, who knew a great deal for somebody who spent all day and going up and down in a lift.

Ever since 3 p.m., a small, annoying biplane had been circling above the West End, its drone somehow seeming to add to the heat of the day. It was evidently too hot for shopping, and on the Furniture and Furnishing Fabrics floor, which was the third floor, May Mitton had only taken three pounds all day. The sun was illuminating in vain the multi-colours of the sofas, divans, cushions and throws; it was also fading the reds, in particular. One sunbeam was aiming directly at what was called the American Sofa, possibly because, like America, it was enormous. It was also largely red, but if the summer carried on in this dazzling vein it would soon be largely pink. May was contemplating putting a throw across the sofa's back: a plain grey one would improve the look of it no end. Mrs Jenkins, her supervisor, would probably have done this already, but Mrs Jenkins had taken the day off; she suffered from migraines. Another assistant was on holiday in Bournemouth, so May had nobody to talk to.

Through the window her view of Tottenham Court Road was obscured by one of the large blue and white flags that proclaimed the name of the store in Deco lettering. The effect was sort of baronial, May thought: celebratory. Well, that must be the intention, but Quarmby & Bates was only a mid-sized department store and not among the most fashionable – not a patch on Dickins & Jones for ladies' fashions or Simpson's for men's, while for truly tasteful furniture Liberty's or Heal's (just up the road) would be the preferred destination. The Liberty fabrics were brighter, the Heal's chairs and tables more elegantly geometric and made of paler wood – very important in 1938.

In June May had marked her first six months in London by buying a small, hexagonal book table from Heal's. She'd felt guilty about this, especially given that she could have saved two pounds by using her Q&B discount to buy one of their own. But the Q&B tables were too boxy and wouldn't go with a Heal's writing table, which was May's next target. May aspired to be a writer. She *was* a writer in that she had recently placed two short stories in the *Red* magazine – and Heal's furniture would help her write better.

All the cars rolling along Tottenham Court Road had their tops down. The buses looked sunburned. May liked watching the way people jumped off them when they were still moving, as if they'd suddenly had enough of the bus and wanted nothing more to do with it. She did wish the flags weren't in the way. The other problem with them, May thought, was the very name they proclaimed: Quarmby & Bates. Quarmby was a strange, wandering name that people tended not to be able to spell, whereas Bates was just too abrupt. May spent a

2

lot of her working days thinking up a second name that would give a more elegant impression: Quarmby & Richardson . . . Quarmby and Davenport's . . . You definitely needed three syllables for the second one.

She had often discussed the matter with her best friend, Eleanor Bancroft. They had come down to London from Halifax together to work at Quarmby & Bates, which was a kind of spin-off from Quarmby's, the one department store in Halifax, Mr Quarmby, a very rich Yorkshireman, having teamed up with Mr Bates, a very rich Londoner. A scheme called the Exchange had been established, by which a promising girl could transfer from one store to the other, and May and Ellie, junior assistants at Quarmby's, had taken the plunge.

They had started in Furnishings, where they had soon been given an unofficial warning for talking too much, and then at the start of June Ellie had been sacked. This was always on the cards: she was too direct with the customers, too northern. 'It's dead comfy,' she might say of a settee, which is what she called sofas. To demonstrate the comfort of a divan the tall Ellie might suddenly flop down on it like a suddenly felled tree.

She had a new job now, in Haberdashery at Selfridges, which she seemed to be enjoying, although Ellie really belonged in Fashion, since she dressed so well, emphasising her graceful height with long, gown-like dresses, flowing coats and loosely tied bows. Well, Ellie was an artist – a painter – or she soon would be, just as May would be a writer. It was important to think good thoughts about Ellie.

May had taken more money but had less fun at work since

3

her friend's departure. She knew herself to be good at selling, an accomplishment she was not very proud of. She had a neat, rather reserved face, like a cat's, and knew a small smile at the right moment could make a big difference. It had certainly made a difference in Halifax when she had assisted in Men's Suits. So she could probably continue at Q&B as long as she wanted – for ever, in fact – and if she signed up to the superannuation scheme, she believed, her life would be effectively over.

May turned from the window; there was movement on the far side of the sunlit floor. Lift girl Ann had stepped out to direct a customer towards May, which was not something Ann would normally do. The customer was a man, which was also quite unusual.

He was weaving his way with distaste through the soft furnishings, and he was not a soft man. It became increasingly obvious that his pale face was skull-like. He seemed to barely restrain himself from booting a tartan pouffe out of his way (and might have stubbed his toe had he done, for there was a 'hidden cabinet' inside it). Ann still lingered, her right hand tentatively raised as if to say, 'Good luck with this one.'

May smiled at the man, and was surprised – quite indignant – when he did not smile back. But he did grudgingly remove his hat, to reveal a shaven head. His dark suit was lifeless; he carried a battered leather dispatch case, with something bulky inside.

'Good afternoon,' he said. 'I'm from Scotland Yard.'

Well, he might just as well have said he was a character from a film – although in a film of the Scotland Yard sort he'd have played the criminal, with that shaved head of his,

4

which was also shaved in the photograph in the wallet he was holding out. Detective Sergeant John Price.

May gave one of her enigmatic small smiles. It was quite lost on Sergeant Price, who was tugging out of his case not what it had been designed to hold – papers – but something surprisingly furry: a swatch of material, thick and woollen.

He laid it on the countertop. It was about 18 inches by 9 and had a striking pattern: dark blue flower shapes on a yellow background, each flower contained in a black, diamond-shaped frame, giving the effect of a trellis. The yellow and black combination immediately reminded May of something, but she couldn't think what. The overall effect suggested moody summer days – or summer being held back by the dark trellis. There was a backing of rather delicate white cotton, which seemed to be cosseting the patterned material. It was a remarkably attractive thing for a policeman to be carrying, although Sergeant Price didn't appear to think so. With arms folded he said, 'I believe the Head of Furnishings—'

'—The floor manager? That's Mrs Jenkins.'

'I gather she's off sick.'

Ann Jones must have told him. She still hadn't retreated to her lift; was shading her eyes from the sun on the far side of the floor.

'I'm afraid you're stuck with me,' May said. 'I've worked here about six months, so I might be able to help.'

'We believe this has been cut off a chair,' said Sergeant Price. 'Do you recognise it?'

'Nobody's cut up any of our moquette, Sergeant. We don't stand for that sort of thing at Quarmby & Bates.'

No smile from the policeman.

'I mean, do you recognise the pattern?'

'I don't think it's one of ours . . . Do you mind?'

He stepped aside to let her pick up the material.

'You must have tried a lot of stores?'

'You're the first,' he said, which was surprising, given the relative smallness of Quarmby's, but his flat tone suggested that in no sense was this a compliment. 'I'm on my way to that bigger shop up the road – what's it called again?'

'Heal's.'

The detective nodded. 'My governor said I might as well call in here on my way.'

'I'm very glad you did, Sergeant Price.'

'It's *Detective* Sergeant, actually.' And he evidently resented being given a task that did not live up to that exalted title.

May handed the material back. 'It's rather nice,' she said. A word floated into her brain. 'It's moquette, isn't it?'

'That word has come up.'

'*Where* has it come up?'

'Back at the station.'

Shortly after her arrival in London, May had been on the Tube looking at a notice placed in one of the panels above the windows that usually accommodated adverts for cigarettes, soap or chocolate. It showed a carriage half obscured by the words, BRITISH MOQUETTE FROM HALIFAX USED THROUGHOUT IN THE CONSTRUCTION OF THIS CAR.

The poster had triggered a certain guilt in May. This fact about her hometown ought not to have come as news to her, but it had. She had *heard* of moquette – she even knew that a couple of the Halifax mills specialised in producing it – but the term had always been slightly opaque, along with others she had seen crudely painted on mill walls or chimneys: words like 'worsteds', 'slubbing', 'shoddy'. She could perhaps blame the incredible complications and subdivisions of woollen textile manufacture, or she could blame her education. The girls at Princess Mary's High School were taught more about London or Paris than they were about Halifax, the object being to *transcend* Halifax.

As a girl May had known that moquette was a sort of carpet-like material, and that it was associated in Halifax with the word 'transport'. But until quite recently she had assumed this meant that the moquette-producing mills made carpets for railway carriages, whereas of course 'moquette' was mainly used for seating, and that notice on the Tube had obviously been referring to the seats, because there was no carpet on Tube carriage floors.

Over her time working on the Furnishings floor, moquette had come a little more into focus. It was a woven fabric, which had its pattern woven into it, whereas other, lighter, woven fabrics, such as the various silks and cottons, might have their patterns printed on them. On the furniture floor the names of these lighter woven fabrics – chiffon, chintz, velvets and so on – came up regularly, whereas only a couple of sofas and armchairs were described as being upholstered in moquette (the American Sofa being one), and they were dowdy pieces whose only merit was durability. It occurred to May for the first time that moquette must be primarily used for public, rather than domestic, seating. 'It's used on train seats, isn't it?' she said, 'as well as on ordinary furniture, I mean?'

7

Price nodded minimally.

'This seems a bit heavier than the moquette we have on the chairs here, so I think it's very likely to have come from a train.'

'We have considered that possibility.'

'And ruled it out?'

'No.'

'Or maybe a bus,' said May, for which helpful suggestion she was rewarded with a heavy stare. What a charmless man Price was. But could he *be* charmed?

'Is it evidence?' May said, in a sort of ingenue tone. 'A clue?'

Now she was not so much in a film called *Price of the Yard* as in a detective story: *The Moquette Mystery*. Perhaps she would come to write it all up, either as true crime or lightly fictionalised. That unlikely prospect faded as Price said, 'Probably not.' But it coalesced again as he said, 'But it might be.'

'How did you come by it, Sergeant? Do tell.' May indicated the so-called Conversation Sofa. This was like a Liberty's Knole sofa, with the same delicate floral brocade – silk, in this case – and high back and sides so you were compressed up against the other person, and it was May's intention to flirt with Sergeant Price. But as she began walking towards it she realised he had not budged, so she was required to return to the counter, which was rather humiliating.

Price removed a paper from his inside pocket. 'Two weeks ago we received this by post. It was sent to the Commissioner.'

The top man, thought May. Not the *commissionaire*. She read the typewritten words:

Please find enclosed a clue to a forthcoming London murder.
Yours faithfully,

Then came a scribble – a rather elegant one, done in violet ink.

'How fascinating,' said May, and she meant it.

Price said, 'It's no doubt some loony.'

The paper was good quality. May held it up. 'No watermark'.

'That was the first thing we looked for.'

'Postmark?'

'Charing Cross.'

Which signified nothing, Charing Cross being, more or less officially, the dead centre of London, the eye of the storm.

'When was it received?'

'A week ago. Thursday, July the twenty-eighth. Posted the day before.'

'Have you connected it to any particular murder?'

'No. There have been three murders in the Metropolitan Police district in the past week . . .'

'Seems rather a lot,' said May, which she probably shouldn't have, since it was tantamount to criticism of the police. 'What sort of murders?'

'I don't want to go into the details.'

May raised her eyebrows.

'You'd only find them distressing.'

'I wouldn't, you know,' May said, adopting an enigmatic expression, as if she might have done a few murders herself.

'Two were what we call domestics,' said Price. 'A husband killed his wife; a wife killed her husband. The other was a drunken fight. All three were in the East End.'

It was hard to see how an unusually attractive moquette might have come into the picture there. Price was now picking up the cloth to stuff it back into his dispatch case, which he absolutely must not do.

'Of course, you'll want to look through our sample books,' May said, indicating the one that happened to be on the counter top and, with a sweep of her arm, the many others dotted around. If he looked at them all he'd be here beyond closing time, as would May, but she must hold on to this real-life mystery. She and Ellie had come to London for adventures. But while they'd had good times – dancing (usually with each other), some nice teas and 'small sherries' (a term they used for minor pleasures like photographing each other in Trafalgar Square with Ellie's box camera) – nothing really exciting had occurred.

'I suppose I should have a quick look,' said Price, and he began leafing through the counter top sample book.

Suddenly, May had a plan. For it to work she must obtain a piece of this blue and gold moquette. It still lay on the counter top. Having given another sample book a perfunctory flip through, Price said, 'I think I can take it as read the material doesn't come from here.'

'The moquette,' May corrected.

'The moquette, yes.'

'Oh, Sergeant Price,' May said, touching his arm. 'I've just had the most wonderful idea. Well, an idea, anyhow. Most of the railway moquette in Britain is made in Halifax, where

I come from. Two mills in particular do moquette, and I know them both.' (The first sentence was probably true. The second was a bit of a lie: she had forgotten the names of the mills.) 'I'm off up to Halifax next week . . .'

She had said 'off up' to emphasise her northern-ness and make her story ring true, and this part *was* true. Quarmby & Bates gave two weeks' paid holiday, and May was going to take her first week from the coming Monday. She had nothing planned except a day trip on Tuesday to see her dad in Halifax. 'If you'd let me have a piece of this moquette, I could take it around the mills, or those two at any rate. Somebody might know something even if they didn't make the moquette themselves, and—'

'That'd be quite irregular, miss,' said Price, but May thought his use of the word 'miss' promising. She knew what to do now: go back on what she'd said. If you offered somebody something and then withdrew it, they invariably wanted it. She'd found the tactic useful when selling.

'Hold on, I'm sorry, I'm being daft, aren't I? You must think I'm crackers. Of course you can't possibly let me have something that might end up as evidence in a murder case. No, you must go to Halifax yourself. It's not like you could show them the moquette over the phone. The trains are quite regular, although you generally have to change at Bradford, and with the through trains you must make sure to be in the right carriage otherwise you'll end up somewhere like Holbeck or Laisterdyke, and once you're in Laisterdyke, it's very hard to get out. There's a fair walk between the mills, and it's mainly uphill wherever you go in Halifax, but there's trams if you can figure out the routes, and there's *usually* a taxi at the station. The folk up there can be a bit stand-offish until they know you, but I'm sure that wouldn't apply to a policeman. I'm ever so sorry for wasting your time with my silly suggestion.'

Sergeant Price looked at her with no noticeable expression for quite a long time. 'Miss, er . . .' he said eventually.

'Mitton.'

'Between you and me, Miss Mitton, I'm not sure why the Yard is pursuing this matter in the first place. Do you know how many loonies write to us every day?'

'No.'

'A lot. So, if you want to take a piece of this . . .'

'Moquette.'

'—up to Halifax with you next week, feel free to do so.'

'And what if I find out anything useful?'

'You could telephone me, I suppose.'

'Only if I know your number.'

He fished for a card, and May stowed it in her purse. 'Have you any scissors lying about?'

2

At half past seven May found Tottenham Court Road Station pleasantly cool after the heat of the road itself. The Northern Line train that carried her home was one of the new ones: bright red on the exterior, jolly as a child's toy. These trains had been subtly cheering her journeys for a few weeks now, but this evening she really thought about them. Inside they were both summery and Christmassy, by virtue of the mainly red and green colours. It occurred to her now that their moquettes, too, were usually red and green. The present one depicted red and green leaves amusingly regimented on vertical branches, upright leaves alternating with inverted ones.

There were only half a dozen other people in the carriage, most of London being on holiday. A smiling man was reading the *Evening News*. It was slightly odd that he was smiling, given the headline: MORE FIGHTING IN FAR EAST.

In the window opposite May, her reflection slid along the soft, fluctuating darkness of the Tube tunnel. When May and Ellie had first come to London they'd found it strange to sit side-on to the direction of travel. It made them laugh, like being on the Waltzer at the fairground. May looked trim and self-contained as usual, her blue eyes with their mysterious glitter of which she was secretly proud. She closed them slowly, cat-like, opened them; the glitter was still there, and she smiled.

Price had let her snip off nearly half the moquette he'd brought with him, and it was now neatly rolled in the bag on her lap. This was her small Gladstone bag, bought for only four shillings from a second-hand store in Camden, but with a gold clasp, and an inside label reading 'Finigan's of Bond Street'. It might almost have been designed to carry the moquette. Also inside it was a copy of the *Listener* she'd bought from the Tottenham Court Road Tube newsagent. Much of the *Listener* was devoted to telling you what to listen to on the wireless, and May read those parts even though she had no wireless. But it also told you what to read, and May had a budget for books and subscriptions to three libraries.

As the train approached Camden she brushed her hand over the vacant seat next to her. The moquette was bristly, and another word floated into her mind: 'pile'. Moquette had a pile: tufts that stood up. She opened her bag and ran her hand over the material inside. The texture was similar to that of the seat – perhaps slightly softer, but she was sure that 'her' moquette must be railway moquette.

The *Evening News* man alighted at Chalk Farm, leaving his paper behind. May picked it up and began flicking through it in search of a murder. She had found none when the train reached her stop, Belsize Park. 'Forthcoming', the anonymous note had said, which – since it was the same word used in connection with films about to be released – gave the bizarre suggestion of something exciting in the offing. In the cinemas, 'forthcoming' meant within a month or so.

Therefore May might have to wait some time for her moquette murder, and when it occurred, how would she know? It also occurred to her to wonder (as she began her ascent of the 291 stairs that led to the ticket hall, the lift having been out of order for the past week) whether the sender of the moquette knew when and where the murder would occur.

Alone on the stairs that circled the great dusty air pipe, she considered the question. Surely the sender was either the boastful and swaggering prospective killer or someone who knew the killer's identity? Had the killer – or the intended victim – made this moquette: woven it, designed it, acquired it for a railway or a bus company? Or did it indicate a murder site?

May was at the mid-point of her ascent, where the groaning of the pipe was at its loudest. From above she heard loud, rapidly descending bootsteps; they became a descending man, dapperly dressed and aggressive-looking. He was not out of breath; he had taken the stairs in his stride, so to speak. So it was not necessary to commiserate with him about the lift being out of order, but he seemed to demand some comment from May, for he stopped his descent and, with accusatory folded arms, stared at her as she passed. When she emerged into the ticket hall, with its smart cream and maroon tiles, May thought, the Underground *had* to be beautiful, to keep up passengers' morale – to mitigate the effect of too many strangers too close together.

The Tube station stood on Rosslyn Hill, a pleasant-enough thoroughfare mainly concerned with taking people up to Hampstead. Off it lay the sleepy houses of Ornan Road, which would bring May out at Belsize Lane, pretty and village-like.

15

Belsize Park was a good area for a shop assistant to be living in, albeit a little faded. 'The Poor Man's Hampstead', it was known as. Girls on the Exchange were given a list of respectable accommodation providers and, as usual, May's luck had been better than Ellie's. She had ended up in a bedsitter in rather crumbling and badly connected Islington, whereas May had the direct line to the West End and two rooms: sitting room and 'Kit-Bath' (kitchen-bathroom).

On Belsize Lane the shops were still open beneath their pale green awnings, the tall trees outside looking perfectly at home on the pavements. The shops were in tall, stately buildings, the shopkeepers and others living above. But May lived *below* a shop, which was the catch, of course, and the reason the rent was only fifteen shillings a week, which she could just about afford. It was a slight humiliation to descend those eight steps to her front door. But at least she *had* her own front door, complete with letter box – and the shop above, Craxton's, was quiet, Mr Craxton being an elderly tailor.

May unlocked the door and accidentally kicked two letters that had been delivered that day. The first could stay kicked. She knew from the size of the envelope that it was a returned manuscript. The customary slip, from *Sunday at Home* magazine, read, 'We have considered your manuscript and regret that it is unsuited to our needs.' Well, it was almost a compliment to be rejected by that dreary lot. She ought to have heeded the warning in *How to Write for Profit* by Robertson Forbes: 'The tone is rather high,' by which he meant priggish. The other letter was from Ellie. May would read it later.

Her rooms were too dark on this sunny evening. She

opened the pale blue curtains as wide as possible, which made no difference. May did not yet think of her rooms as 'home' in the fullest sense of the word. Her attempts to make the rooms her own had stalled after the purchase of the book table, whose elegance upstaged everything else. She had recently realised that her other major purchase, the rather modern grey and black rug, wasn't modern *enough* and only added to the gloom. She liked the yellow on the yellow and pink counterpane she'd brought down from Halifax, but not the pink, and even the yellow wasn't as good as the yellow of 'her' moquette. She took it from the Gladstone bag and stretched it out on the book table. Was it a blessing or a curse? It held the promise of an adventure, but also the promise of a murder.

The evening sunlight reached only as far as the gas fire and the gas and electric meters above it. Why weren't the meters in the kit-bath where all the other embarrassing devices were congregated? The kit-bath was more like an alcove than a room. It lay behind a kind of arch hung with a beaded curtain of melodramatic, glittery black. Every time May walked through it she felt like Mata Hari.

Of course no guests were ever permitted into the kit-bath, because of the 'bath' part of it, although she'd hardly had any guests apart from Ellie. Her dad had come down twice, and she had once brought around the young man, Carl, who'd been *her* 'young man' (for about three weeks), the assistant book buyer at Q&B. May had thought they would have literature in common, but it seemed Carl never read the books he bought for Q&B. Because of their break-up the book floor was out of bounds to May, but she was used to having to dodge young men it was no longer convenient to run into. Halifax had been littered with them.

Tea was a tin of cod roes, bread and butter, an apple and a glass of milk. She ate it on the pine table, which was also her desk, with her dark green 'Royal' portable typewriter next to the sugar bowl. Halfway through, she lit a candle rather than put a shilling in the electric. That way she could carry on reading the *Listener* in comfort. She must look out for a few 'forthcoming titles': *Miss Pettigrew Lives for a Day* looked good, especially since she, Miss Mitton, was planning to live for at least a day herself.

After her tea, May ran the bath. On the little wicker chair she kept beside it, she placed the candle, half a bar of Nestle's chocolate cream, another glass of milk, the letter from Ellie and the one bath cube she had left. May loved hot baths, no matter how hot the weather, and there must always be enough money in the meter for them, hence cold teas.

In the bath, she opened Ellie's letter. It was short.

Thursday

Dearest May Kitten,

Nothing has occurred. NOWT. Haven't even been sacked yet. In fact, took eleven pounds today. Heard nothing from AJ, of course. Pushing his luck with the long silences, is that boy. Maybe he didn't care for the sketch I sent him of himself not writing a letter. He did look rather gormless in it.

As you know, I'm off to Scarborough Fair next week and things have been known to happen in Scarborough, I believe,

18

altho not usually with one's folks in tow. Anyhow, sketches
will be sketched, the castle will be painted at sunset, sunrise,
by moonlight and (how about this for a change?) THE
CASTLE JUST BEFORE TEATIME.

But that's not till Tues and on Mon I have a drawing class
at Morley College – 271 Westminster Bridge Road, round
t'back of Waterloo. It's a life class, which means I will be
drawing a person – probably male – who is alive, but not
(please God) naked. Knocks off at half-seven. They have a
canteen where service is speedy and chipped potatoes and
chicken pie is sixpence with pudding thrown in, sometimes
quite literally. Then we cd repair around t' corner to THE
LAMBETH TAVERN or something like that for <u>extremely</u>
small sherries, or maybe I'll have a pint of beer and you can
pretend you're not with me. How about it, kidder?

Love,
EB

May would be there on Monday.

She twisted the hot tap with her toe, for more nearly
boiling water – she liked the noise of it glugging in as well
as the heat.

The 'folks' in Ellie's letter were not her parents but her
aunt Sarah and uncle Dick. May's mother, like Ellie's, was
dead, but even in this melancholic conjunction May had come
off best, since she had been 15 when her mother died whereas
Ellie had been seven – and Ellie had never known her father.
As for 'AJ', that was Anthony Johnson, a cautious solicitor's
clerk likely to end up a solicitor (a bald one, thought May,

recalling his looks). He'd been Ellie's 'boy' in Halifax, despite having precisely the opposite personality. He'd been down to London twice to see her, but it didn't seem likely he'd been coming again. Ellie could and would do better.

After her bath May took the novel she had on the go, *Cakes and Ale* by Somerset Maugham, to bed with her. She wanted to learn the secrets of Maugham, who had made a fortune from his writing, but she kept glancing over to the *Evening News* on her book table, and eventually she got out of bed to fetch it. It looked different by candlelight – more redolent of London mysteries – and there, on page six, was a small item she'd not noticed on the Tube.

MISSING TRAIN DRIVER

North London police are appealing for information in connection with the disappearance from the vicinity of King's Cross Station of an engine driver. Mr Dougal Byrne, 62, a 'top link' driver for the London and North Eastern Railway, was last seen at midnight on Monday walking from the engine men's mess adjacent to the King's Cross Locomotive Shed into the Goods Yard. He was reported missing by his wife, Mrs Marjorie Byrne, 59, of Caledonian Road the following morning. Anyone with information is requested to communicate with Scotland Yard.

Perhaps they would be lucky enough to speak to Detective Sergeant Price himself, thought May. She wondered if he associated this railway disappearance, which might yet become a railway murder, with the piece of material that was very likely a piece of railway moquette. Granted, the article lying beside her Gladstone bag seemed to signify comfort, whereas Mr Dougal Byrne worked at the dirty and dangerous end of a train. But surely such a man tasted railway luxury occasionally, especially given that he was of the 'top link' (whatever that meant)? His disappearance had occurred within – what? – five days of the sending of the 'clue' to the police, a plausible sort of interlude.

May blew out her candle, but it was not so easy to terminate her speculations.

3

On Friday, another hot day, May took four pounds, most of it through the sale of a rollback chair. In what was officially her 'lunch break', but which May, being northern, considered her 'dinner break', she learned from the *Evening News* that 'an extensive police search' for Mr Dougal Byrne had commenced.

The Saturday was hotter still; commensurately the shop was even quieter, and she took barely three pounds. She didn't know why Quarmby & Bates bothered to stay open on summer Saturday afternoons. Most London stores did not. At least it closed early, so the sun was still bright when, at six o'clock, May's holiday began.

After clocking off, she walked to King's Cross Station with a twofold purpose: to buy tickets for Halifax, and to find out something about Mr Dougal Byrne. There had been nothing about him in that afternoon's *Evening News*, but they would surely report him found, alive or dead. The paper would be hoping for the latter, of course. It was troubling to reflect that, for her adventure to begin, Mr Byrne must die.

May always tried to buy railway tickets in advance: it gave you the excitement associated with the journey twice over. The booking hall was overheated and filled with cigarette smoke, occasionally supplemented by wafts of steam. Posters behind the clerks blazoned sophisticated-looking people lounging on beaches of dazzling yellow, which turned out to be in Yorkshire. You hoped they'd got sun lotion to hand. Well, she could have a day at the seaside as well as her trip to Halifax, she thought, stowing her tickets in her purse. Her week off needn't be all about moquette.

The goods yard and locomotive shed occupied a sprawling territory behind the station, the railway backstage as it were. Gradually May became the only woman amid a cohort of sooty-looking men, most in blue overalls and oily caps. Ahead of her the slight pinkness of a hot early evening was being stained by plumes of grey steam and threads of black smoke rising from beyond a high wall. The gates stood open but were guarded a sort of languid sentry in the doorway of an adjacent brick lodge. He wore a railwayman's uniform but with a tie that must have been against regulations, being orange with large blue spots. His cap sat atop a great crest of brilliantined hair, and his moustache was neatly divided like Clark Gable's. 'Flash', was the word. May did not anticipate any difficulty obtaining information from him. He smiled broadly. 'All right, love? How can I help you?'

Over his right shoulder she could see a man at a desk and a green baize noticeboard on which official documents were pinned alongside a photograph of Barbara Stanwyck.

'I do like your tie,' said May.

'Thank you, love. I wish you'd tell my governor. He thinks it makes me look *a right Nancy*!' and he shouted those last three words with a twist of his head, presumably towards the man at the desk.

'I'm awfully sorry to bother you,' said May, 'but I was wondering about that poor Mr Byrne, the fellow who'd disappeared.'

'Oh, yes? Are you related to him, love?'

May couldn't bring herself to pretend that she was, so she said, 'Oh, no. Just curious. I've been reading about him in the paper, and as I was passing by I thought I'd ask after him. I do hope he's all right.'

A certain suspicion had crept into the rascally man's appraisal of May. '*Why* were you passing by, if you don't mind my asking, love?'

May pointed to a sign fixed to the wall alongside the gate. 'My young man works in the Fish and Coal Office.'

The man smirked. 'I'll bet you lead him an awful dance.'

'Will you leave off chatting up the girl, Len,' shouted the man at the desk, 'and get these blinking dockets done.'

'Duty calls, miss,' said the sentry. 'Fact is, we know nothing beyond what's been in the papers.' He gestured towards the goods yard, beyond which hung the grey haze that presumably denoted massed locomotives. 'It's quite easy to come a cropper in there.'

May gazed at the lines of wagons – miles and miles of them, it seemed, most containing coal; small locomotives moved on the tracks in between like patrolling prison wardens. Every so often one of the engines would bash a line of wagons for no apparent reason, unless to maintain the echoing jangle that hung in the air. Wires or cables were held on giant cotton wheels, dangerously stacked; if one shifted an inch the whole lot would go bouncing and rolling down between the trains. There were great cliff faces of bales and bundles. Barn-like buildings with roofs but no walls were big enough to harbour entire trains, or stuffed with further mysterious contraband. There was a great, ugly concrete tower resembling a fat, bow-legged man, and an engine waiting underneath for some no doubt monstrously noisy and dirty event to occur. This was a world away from fancy moquette.

'Course, there has been a few rumours . . .'

'Such as?'

'He was – shouldn't say that – a difficult sort of chap to get on with. Habit of falling out with his mates.'

'With his friends, you mean?'

'His firemen, love. Rows on the footplates. Couple of years back he came to blows with a mate when they were coming back on the cushions—'

'The *cushions*? How do you mean?'

'At the end of a turn the footplate blokes might come back as passengers. That's called being on the cushions.'

'Where were they coming back from?'

'Don't know. Peterborough, maybe?'

'Do you know the name of the man he had a row with?'

It was a question too far.

'Maybe I do, and I maybe I don't. Why do *you* want to know, love? And while we're on the subject of names, what's yours? And come to that, what's the name of your boyfriend in the Fish and Coal? I don't see you walking out with some little clerk. You're a bit too mysterious for that, and a bit too—'

'*Len!*' yelled the man in the lodge. 'For God's sake leave off with the girl, will you!'

'Perhaps I'll come back later,' said May.

'You do that, love,' said Len, smiling. 'I'm here most days till seven.'

Back at King's Cross, a poster reading 'Enjoy the Fresh Air and Bovril Sandwiches' inspired May to purchase a sandwich (cheese, not Bovril) and a lemonade from the coffee stall on the forecourt. She liked how this stall was lit by naphtha flares at night, giving a fairground atmosphere. In their first London weeks it had been a meeting place for her and Ellie. The stallholder, a small, possibly Italian man with a slightly bedraggled bow tie nodded when May asked if she could leave her half-consumed meal on the counter while she went to get a newspaper. She bought the *Evening Standard* by way of a change from the *News*, and a flash of red on the back page caught her eye: in smudgy print, not quite centred, STOP PRESS.

> Artist Rex Braddon, 57, found dead with gun-shot wound at Maida Vale flat. Scotland Yard called in.

The disappearance of Byrne had suggested a railway murder but probably not an artistic one. Here, perhaps, was the opposite scenario.

Rex Braddon must be famous to have merited the red print, but May had never heard of him. Writers were her line. Ellie would probably know of him, though. Braddon had been 'found dead'. So he could have been dead for days – probably not weeks, though – in sedate-sounding Maida Vale. There was something of the Victorian funeral about those two words. May consulted her *London Underground Railway Map* folded in her purse. How she loved this little map, with its elegant red and grey cover. Whereas the austere maps in the stations showed the Tube as a world of its own, this one showed the lines coexisting amiably with parks and 'principal thoroughfares'. She found Maida Vale hovering just left of Edgware Road and not much further out than Marylebone. It was on the Bakerloo Line, which she could reach by taking the Piccadilly Line from the Tube Station to her left, a purple building with tearoom and tobacconist's attached, and a general air of asserting its own identity against the bigger station looming behind.

Down on the cool platform one of the red trains was waiting, but instead of the red and green leaf moquette this one had quite a complex tartan – like one tartan superimposed on another. It was mainly green and brown, but a thin, bright red line was what you really noticed, and it testified to the wit of the design.

At Piccadilly Circus, she found herself walking against a happy tide of people, this being the end of the working week with fine weather waiting above. The Bakerloo Line had old trains that were noisier and more industrial-looking and with forgettable colours. The moquette inside the one she boarded had slightly blurry rectangles in workaday blue and brown.

Maida Vale Station, on the other hand, was artistic, a little jewellery box with red, green and cream tiles. The stairs had fancy banisters, and the Tube circle-and-bar was done as a mosaic smiling down on everything. May emerged into Elgin Avenue, which consisted of tall, respectable houses, and the warm air was impregnated with the sweet, countrified smell from a greengrocer's. The boy selling newspapers outside the station was still peddling the fighting in the Far East. Didn't he know that Maida Vale had its very own drama? 'Excuse me,' May asked him, 'but hasn't a murder happened near here?'

'It has,' he said, with an unpleasant smile.

'Could you tell me exactly where?'

'I can,' he said. The smile remained. May wondered if she ought to buy a paper. But the boy was merely savouring his morbid disclosures. 'A fellow was shot.'

'Today?'

'Don't think so. Only they *found* him today – just round the corner.'

'That street there?' May said, pointing to the one she thought the boy had indicated.

'First left off it. You can't miss.'

'Thanks.'

'—Because of all the coppers.'

4

But there was only one copper. He stood outside a large house on a street called Grantully Gardens, and there was indeed a small garden or park opposite. The policeman was being addressed by another man, but still looking straight ahead, and he didn't even shake his head as the man said, 'Is there another officer I might speak to about this?'

What the policeman was actually staring at was a big hole in the road, partly covered with tarpaulin. Gravel and mud was piled up beside it. An excavator had its bucket scoop upraised and curled in towards the cab like a bird sleeping with its head under its wing. Paraffin burners glowed gently on portable railings around the hole, their blue radiance vivid against the darkening blue of the sky, in which there was just enough light to see accumulating black clouds. The rain began quite suddenly and noisily, soft warm drops.

The enquirer turned away from the policeman and caught May's eye. He ran his hand through his thick dark hair. He was hatless, perhaps to show off the hair, although he did not seem the show-off type, despite being rather handsome and well-dressed: dark trousers, loose white linen jacket: pale blue shirt front with white starchy collar of the old-fashioned sort (round edges). His tie was strange, though: something between a drooping bow tie and a loosely knotted ribbon. The effect was somehow American. Had he spoken with an American accent? it was partly to find out that May asked him, 'Is this where the murder happened?'

The young man looked away while scratching the back of his neck, which probably didn't need scratching. 'Uh-huh,' he said, which did indicate Americanness. He was thin and somewhat nervous-looking, with large brown eyes. When he brushed his hair back again he didn't look completely unlike an actor May had taken a liking to in a film she'd seen last year or so, *The Petrified Forest*. An American film of course, like most. Humphrey Bogart was the name. This rather promising stranger looked to be in his early twenties, a little older than May.

'You must think I'm one of those ghouls,' she said.

He shook his head in a charmingly emphatic way. 'You don't look ghoulish, miss.'

'Did you know the man? I'm sorry if so.'

'Nu-uh.' A variant on 'Uh-huh', it seemed. Suddenly he smiled and extended his hand. 'Tom Crosby.'

'May Mitton,' and they shook. She was always curious about the effect of her name. People usually made some comment about it. She was glad Tom Crosby did not say, 'I like the way both names begin with "M".' Book-buyer Carl had said that, and he hadn't much liked it when May had said, 'It's called alliteration.'

Tom Crosby gestured to the guarded door. 'I had a conversation with him once.'

'The murdered man? Might I ask about what?'

'Oh, you know, railways . . . trains.' He smiled suddenly again.

'But I thought he was an artist?' said May, hoping her racing heart was not evident in her voice.

'Uh-huh. An artist who worked for the railways. On occasion.'

'What railways?'

'London Underground. The Southern. And I think he did things for the LNER – London & North Eastern.'

They were the King's Cross lot, thought May, probably the ones who would be taking her to Halifax on Tuesday; also the ones Dougal Byrne worked for. 'What did he do for them?'

'Oh, posters – maybe a book cover, or two.' Crosby smiled again. 'Can't beat the train.'

'No indeed.' May was somewhat baffled.

'It's a slogan. The one on the poster he did for them. It showed a car racing a train. The car was winning.' That sudden smile again. 'We're getting *rained on* here.

'I had noticed that.'

'Shall we head back to . . .'

Back to where? May wondered, but she was walking alongside him anyway.

'I like your bag,' he said.

'Thanks. It's a Gladstone bag.'

'I know. It's neat.'

'Are you American?'

'Only slightly. Born in New York; left when I was seven. Ever been to New York, May?'

She had, but only in her imagination, fired by hundreds of films. 'I haven't even been to *old* York, which is pretty

31

remiss of me considering I was born about forty miles away in Halifax.'

'I've been to York,' he said. 'York *Station* – principal traffic centre for the North, with the possible exception of Carlisle. I've also been to Halifax Old station, which is not particularly old, as I'm sure you know. And I've been to Halifax North Bridge, *and* the other one. What's it called?'

'Halifax St Paul's.'

'Bingo.'

'Nobody goes there.'

'I've been twice.'

'What are you? A train driver?'

'Ha!' he said, quite loudly. 'Wouldn't *that* be fine?'

He seemed to be imagining it as they walked. Meanwhile, May was wondering whether to tell him about Dougal Byrne. But no; she must find out more about Tom Crosby first. Eventually, he said, 'I work on a railway magazine, May.'

'You're a journalist?' She very much hoped so, but of course he could just be a clerk or an accountant or something.

'Uh-huh. Special Correspondent. Also, the *only* correspondent.'

'I noticed your correspondent shoes,' said May and he laughed a really delighted laugh, albeit without quite looking at her. She now noticed the rolled-up magazine in his jacket pocket.

They were back on Elgin Avenue, the Underground station glowing prettily across the road, but Tom Crosby was looking further along. 'There's *that*,' he said, indicating a pub. 'We could . . . get out of the rain.'

'Yes, let's,' said May, who'd had enough of being coy.

The pub was moderately crowded with people escaping the rain – sporty young men and women with jumpers over their shoulders. It was smart, with stained glass windows and wall tiles with pale green leaf patterns. Tom Crosby asked what she would like to drink, and for the first time ever she said the words 'A small sherry, please' in all seriousness. The barman who came up to Tom Crosby said, 'Hello again, sir,' which caused May a flicker of anxiety. He hadn't mentioned that he'd been in the pub before, but then he hadn't had the chance to.

'Same again, sir?' said the barman, compounding the worry. 'Pint of mild?'

Tom nodded. As they walked over to a table May said, 'Do they have that in America?'

'Warm, dark, weak beer? They do not, May. But the way I see it, it's their loss.' They clinked glasses, which seemed an odd thing to do in the aftermath of a murder.

'Why did you leave America? Sorry for asking all these questions.'

'That's perfectly all right. I have a few lined up for you, too. It was Dad who left. Mom and I left with him.'

'And why did *he* leave?'

Tom Crosby fished in his pocket, the one without the magazine, producing cigarettes and a small, stylish lighter. The cigarettes were Star brand, which May had never seen before. The packet showed a grey star on an orange background and was highly attractive, but then so were most cigarette packets. He offered her one and May surprised herself by taking it. This would be the third cigarette she had ever smoked. 'Oh, hiding from people,' he said, answering the question she'd almost forgotten she'd asked. 'His creditors. Since the smash, you know. Dad makes cars. Ever heard of the Huntsville Arrow?'

May shook her head.

'That's one of Dad's. It looks real nice – and it breaks down a lot.' He lit her cigarette. She liked his hairy, thin wrists, and the gold watch with rectangular face, as trim as the lighter.

'But your own interest is in the railways?'

'Uh-huh. Well, sort of. It would be more accurate to say that the magazine I work for is interested in railways.' He blew smoke, as did May, less expertly. 'Why are you interested in Rex Braddon, May?'

The sudden change in tone seemed almost rude, but then again, his curiosity was natural in the circumstances, and his tone had only changed because he'd been exceptionally polite up to now. May had placed the Gladstone bag on an adjacent empty seat. She lifted it onto her knee while trying to think of a casual, conversational way of introducing the moquette. 'To cut a long story short,' she said, 'I've been given what might be a clue to his murder.'

She obviously hadn't succeeded in her attempt to be casual, for this news seemed to fairly stun Tom Crosby. He laid his cigarette down in the ashtray with a hand that was possibly shaking. He brushed his hair back with the hand that had held the cigarette. He folded his arms and looked down at his shoes. When he looked at May again – or nearly looked at her – there was a half-smile on his face.

'This piece of moquette,' she said, holding it up.

'Is it railway moquette?' he said. 'I believe I might recognise it. May I?'

She handed it over to him.

'No,' he said, quickly offering it back. 'No, I don't.' He drank his beer – quite a lot of it – then, 'You've given me the *short* story, May. I'd like to hear the longer one.'

She couldn't do so, she found, without supplying much ancillary detail about her life. Before she got to Sergeant Price there was a great Halifax preamble about how she came to be at Quarmby & Bates in the first place, and Halifax cropped up again when she set about telling how she was going to be pursuing her 'inquiries'. She tried to assume a light tone here, adopting Price's line that the moquette had almost certainly been sent to the Yard by a loony.

Tom Crosby nodded, exhaling smoke and looking to the left. She did wish he would look at her more. It was very evident that their glasses were empty, and the rain had stopped; they were free to go. But Tom said, 'Care for another one, May?'

When he returned from the bar, he said, 'Braddon . . . My turn.'

About six weeks ago, it seemed, he had interviewed Braddon for his magazine, for an article 'pegged', as he put it, to a retrospective exhibition of Braddon's work coming up at a London gallery. Braddon was worth interviewing for a railway magazine: as well as railway posters he had designed covers for big-selling Southern Railway publications.

'Do you think he designed moquettes?' said May.

Tom shrugged. 'Artists do these days. But it never came up in our talk – and we went over his career pretty thoroughly.'

Evidently Tom had not been invited into Braddon's flat,

which was on the ground floor of the building. Instead, they had strolled and talked in the garden opposite.

'Was the interview published?'

'Nope.'

'Why not?'

'He wanted to see the piece beforehand. He wanted copy approval, May. No journalist can agree to that.'

'I suppose that would have put you off. But did you like him to begin with?'

Tom ran his hands through his hair. 'As a man?'

'Yes.'

'Not especially.'

'As an artist?'

'Same again, but I'm no art critic.'

'What would I know by him?'

'Let me see . . . He did some panels for the Tube carriages telling you to take your litter home.'

May thought she'd seen those: amusing drawings of a sort of pin-headed couple sitting in a carriage with a mound of rubbish at their feet. The man looked like Stan Laurel. She described this to Tom, who shook his head.

'That's Fougasse. He's good – witty. Braddon's version is heavier. You'd *better* take your litter home with you, or you'll be fined, sort of thing.'

'And you never saw him again after your talk in the garden?'

'Nope.'

'What brought you here tonight?'

'Morbid curiosity, I guess.'

May said, 'You saw the stop press item?'

Tom was nodding. 'Came straight by at about five.'

'Is that why the barman said, "Hello again" when he saw you?'

'Just now was my second visit to the crime scene. I looked in here after the first. Seemed a good place to kill time while I waited for the new cop.'

'The new cop?'

'I thought he might be more informative than the first. Turned out to be less. The first one wasn't exactly friendly, but he did talk. He told me some things.'

'*What* did the cop tell you?' May asked – partly for the sake of saying 'cop'.

Tom Crosby lit another cigarette. What he'd learned, he told her, was that Braddon had been shot two or three days ago by a light-calibre weapon, the sound of the shot perhaps drowned out by the noisy roadworks. No witnesses had yet come forward. There were four flats in the building. Crosby had been shot in the first-storey one, which he owned and lived in. (The police knew he'd been shot by a third party, rather than shooting himself, because there was no gun found in the flat.) Braddon also owned the flat below and the flat above, both of which he sometimes let on short leases, but both had been untenanted for months. Clearly he didn't need the money. He owned other flats in London besides these three. The top floor flat was tenanted, but the owner was away on holiday, like half the residents of Maida Vale.

There was a sort of alleyway through the gardens that led from the side door of the building where Braddon lived to the main road behind, Elgin Avenue. That was the killer's likely means of escape. A neighbour thought they had heard someone running along there one afternoon two days ago, but they'd been concealed by the hedge.

Then the cop had 'clammed up', seemingly regretting talking in the first place. Tom had then tried the second cop, with the result May had seen.

There was a lot in what she'd just learned that May would have liked to discuss further. She also wanted to ask Tom about the magazine in his pocket, but she felt she had reached the limit of permissible questions. They agreed to travel some of the way home together – as far as Piccadilly Circus, where she would change for the Northern Line, Tom for the Piccadilly that would carry him 'west' (he seemed a little vague about where he lived, but then so had May been).

In Maida Vale Station, May remarked on the beauty of the architecture. Tom said it was the work of a man with the un-beautiful name of Stanley Heaps, following on from the style of a man called Leslie Green, Chief Architect of Charles Yerkes, founder of the original Underground company, the Underground Electric Railways of London.

May had heard of Yerkes. 'He was American, wasn't he?'

'It's all American, May,' Tom said, gesturing at the 'Underground' mosaic above them, the extravagant green and gold illumination. 'The way the lines go "Northbound" and "Southbound" instead of "Up" and "Down", which was always the British way. The carriages are "cars", the guards are "conductors".' But he didn't seem to be boasting about the achievements of his fellow countrymen. He seemed almost to regret their intrusion into London life.

They were on the 'down' escalator. Two middle-aged

women were passing by on the 'up' one, and brazenly staring. They would be connoisseurs of young couples, thought May, and she wondered what they were making of her and Tom Crosby. They would probably be noting that, as he spoke, Tom did not often meet May's eye. They would have him down as shy, maybe arrogant. They would *surely* have him down as handsome, though. As for herself? A watchful girl, proud, rather primly pretty. They would be able to tell that the two of them had only just met, and May wondered whether Tom Crosby would always seem like the kind of person you'd only just met.

As the train came in Tom asked if she'd mind sitting in a smoker. She did not. Her father, who had once been a heavy smoker himself, had advised her: 'The smokers will look after you, love.' For a moment May didn't know whether Tom was going to sit next to her or opposite; she didn't believe he knew, either. To make him sit next to her she pointed at his pocket. 'Is that your magazine?'

'Here you go,' he said as they sat down side-by-side. There was a boring picture of a train on the cover. She read the title out loud: 'The *Railway Digest*.'

'I know, I know,' he said, taking his cigarettes from his pocket. 'It sounds like a kind of biscuit you'd get in a dining car.'

'"Incorporating the *English and Scottish Railway Herald*."'

'Which ceased publication in 1913. And with good reason, May.'

They stopped at Warwick Avenue. Tom was watching her so closely as she leafed through the magazine that she felt obliged to say things, but she couldn't think what. It was very technical. A column illustrated by a small cartoon of a woman reading on a train (the only woman featured in the whole thing, as far as May could make out) offered some light relief. It was headlined 'Something sensational . . .', and what followed was a book review – of *Stamboul Train*, by Graham Greene, which May had not read, but knew had been a Book Club choice a few years back, which was very good news for Graham Greene. The review was signed 'Tom Crosby'. It seemed favourable, concluding, '. . . and here's hoping the estimable Mr Greene takes another train soon.' Under the review came the words, '. . . To Read on the Train', a continuation of the headline. It was a quote from something, she was sure: 'You must always have something sensational to read in the train.'

'That's my first innovation,' Tom said. 'Reviews of books normal people might want to read. Books to read *on* trains rather than about them.'

They were at Paddington. She had come to a page headlined, 'The Main-Line Gradients of French Railways, Part 2.'

'But this magazine is *not* for normal people, is it?'

Tom gave a sort of agitated laugh. 'But I'm going to change it. First the title, then everything else.'

'What would you call it?'

'What *will* I, May. The *Railway Express*.'

'Like the *Daily Express*?'

'The best-selling newspaper in Britain, May. Why? Because it deals in news. It says, "Here's something you didn't know", and it dares you to ignore it. Do you know what happened last month on the railways?'

'A lot of things, I should imagine.'

'An engine of the London & North Eastern Railway, *Mallard*, broke the world speed record for steam.'

'Yes, I heard of that. Why's it called *Mallard*? A mallard's a duck.'

'Well, May, ducks are beautiful things in flight.'

'I suppose they are.'

'And the designer of the engine, Sir Nigel Gresley, likes shooting them.'

'I knew there must be some good reason.'

He smiled, but his intensity did not relent. 'A hundred and twenty-six miles an hour, May! Our report's in the next edition. You know what our cover line is? It's in extra-small type, incidentally – twelve-point.'

May shrugged. She liked his terminology.

'"LNER break test successful". Because they *were* testing the brakes, but the main thing they were doing is smashing the world record held by the damn Germans, May. Now don't you think that needs more than twelve-point?' He perhaps assumed she knew what 12-point was because she'd mentioned that she was an aspiring writer.

'To change this magazine,' she said, 'wouldn't you have to be the editor?'

He nodded to himself for a while, as if turning the matter over. 'Don't know, May. He's not a bad old boy, old Williams – but we have new proprietors, and they want new readers.' Tom was obviously very wrapped up in journalism and in talking about journalism. He hadn't yet lit his cigarette, and they were coming into Piccadilly Circus.

This was 'their' stop, but there was a wide distance between them as they walked along a corridor following signs reading, 'To Northern and Piccadilly Lines'. Soon it would be either or, and May was wondering how they would say goodbye. It was necessary that she must see this man again, but it was not her place to say so, and she worried that he lacked the poise or polish to suggest another meeting even if he wanted one, which on balance she suspected he did.

At the parting of the ways Tom scratched the back of his neck. May waited until he stopped, at which he put both hands in his jacket pockets.

'I'm going this way, you're going that,' May pointed out. This ought to be the other way about, with May being mysterious, which was her speciality.

'Yes,' he said, 'Well, keep the magazine!' and he laughed, not very convincingly.

May took her time putting the magazine in her bag. Londoners flowed past them, bored, laughing, introspective, all looking too hot.

'Well, bye, May,' said Tom, showing her the palm of his right hand, as if signalling goodbye from a distance. A feeling of total contempt for him came over her, until he said, 'Will you let me know if you discover anything?'

May nodded, but it had been a rather half-hearted invitation, especially given that she probably *wouldn't* discover anything. It was partly to detain Tom Crosby that she said, 'Did you read about the disappearance of a train driver?'

Evidently he had not, so May explained about Dougal Byrne, with a brief account of her visit to the King's Cross backstage.

'You know, May,' Tom Crosby said, 'that sounds like a better lead than the shooting of Braddon.'

'But it's not a murder.'

'Not yet, but if there'd been a fight on your moquette, then it does amount to a definite clue that some screwball might want to publicise, for whatever reason. I mean, it could signify a definite time and place. Railway moquettes come and go at a pretty great rate—'

'What sort of rate?'

'Well, they don't change every year, but they might change every two or three.'

Again his response was disappointing. She had been rather hoping he would chivalrously offer to accompany her, should she decide to pick up where she'd left off with lecherous Len at King's Cross.

He raised his right palm in salutation again, and she watched him walk away, liking the way he hunched his shoulders as he lit a cigarette before turning left. But as she headed towards the Piccadilly Line, her doubts accumulated. May considered herself quite a good psychologist where young men were concerned, but she couldn't make him out. Was he too interested in the killing of Max Braddon or not sufficiently? He appeared to have turned up at the scene of the crime at the first opportunity, and he had admitted to a grievance against Braddon. And he had apparently sought to deflect May from looking into the matter, promoting instead the Byrne 'lead', as he had called it. Yes, he had asked to be kept informed of the progress of her inquiries, but was that any more than politeness required? Insofar as he was genuinely interested, might it only be to see whether the trail led towards *him*?

As her Piccadilly Line train hurtled into the platform it presented the usual succession of illuminated people: each one an offer to be accepted or declined. Who were you willing to sit next to? On a sparsely occupied train like this a careful choice must be made, and it occurred to May as she stepped aboard that, for all his attractions, it might be foolish to be voluntarily alone with the mysterious Tom Crosby.

5

May loved the West End. It was like a cross between a funfair and a carnival, and it was always outrageous. Leicester Square itself, for instance, was a garden surrounded by cinemas. You noticed the cinema by night, the garden by day.

It was Monday, which May considered the start of her holiday proper, since she was at large when most people weren't. The day before she had bought the *News of The World* – it was the murder paper after all – but it had nothing about either Dougal Byrne or Rex Braddon, so she'd had to gamble again, since she couldn't afford to buy all the Sunday papers. In the *Observer* she found:

> Scotland Yard detectives are investigating the apparent murder of a well-known artist. The body of Mr Rex Braddon, who had sustained a gunshot wound to the chest, was found at his Maida Vale flat yesterday morning. The discovery was made by Mr Joseph Rogers, caretaker, after Mr Braddon's mail had gone uncollected for several days. An inquest will be held tomorrow.

Mr Braddon, who was 63, was known particularly for the posters and other publicity
material he had designed for London Transport
and other railway companies. He was also a
noted portrait painter, who exhibited regularly
in the London galleries.

It hadn't really got her any further.

There had been a pleasant bustle this sunny morning
about the shops of Belsize Lane, where she'd gone to buy a
bread roll for her bacon butty, that Yorkshire delicacy, and
as she'd passed the florists she'd seen a lovely yellow flower
in the window. Mimosa, apparently: inspired by the partial
yellowness of 'her' moquette May had bought a small bunch.
It wasn't merely pretty: it generated its own light, a floral
emissary of the sun. She considered it a symbol of a London
life that was finally starting. That was down to the moquette.
The principal excitement, of course, had been meeting Tom
Crosby. Surely he couldn't have murdered Rex Braddon over
such a small matter as an argument about the use of a magazine
article? For all his apparent strangeness he had seemed kind.
He had twice bought her drinks, offered her a cigarette, asked
whether she minded being in a 'smoker' on the Tube . . .

She had put the mimosa in her blue glass vase, which was
flower-like itself, cooked herself a butty and given a little
thought to her competition entry. At Quarmby & Bates a staff
circular had announced a prize of three pounds (or at any
rate a three-pound voucher) for a slogan of not more than ten
words promoting the store as 'unisex'. That had been the very
word used, which just showed how fast Q&B was sailing away

46

from its Yorkshire counterpart. The aim was to get couples to come in together, because so often a lone woman would back off from a purchase at the last moment mumbling, 'I'll have to see what my husband thinks.'

She had put on her teal and grey tea dress, which had a short simple jacket fitted to it – a sort of bolero jacket – and, though she ought really to be wearing a brimmed hat on a day like today, her pill box hat, and set off along Ornan Road muttering 'Not I, but we, at Q&B'. That was the best she'd been able to come up with so far. At the Tube she found the lift working. 'You and Me at Q&B', she said, as she descended. *But is that strictly grammatical?* The red train that came in had a rather hazy orangey moquette: the first one on a red train that she hadn't really cared for.

'Quarmby & Bates, Where Marrieds are not Harried' – but that wasn't much of a boast. Marrieds jolly well ought *not* to be harried. Above the window opposite was an advert for Fry's chocolate beside one of the smaller Underground posters. A couple sat on a train, rubbish scattered at their feet. They were overlooked – literally overshadowed – by two officials in long coats and peaked caps. Speech bubbles coming out of these men's mouths had merged into one: 'Take your litter home!' and there was a footnote about a fine. This was the 'heavy' poster by Rex Braddon, the one mentioned by Tom Crosby. It made you realise how charming the usual Underground messages were.

The grass in Leicester Square was parched, and as many people as possible were sitting on the low wall around the fountain: businessmen with newspapers, young mothers with children, a tramp or two. So May walked for a while until she was looking at a great cavalcade proceeding around a bend: Regent Street. She passed the windows of Galeries Lafayette – another place you noticed mainly at night, when those too-lifelike French mannequins were illuminated by unnatural light as they smiled, sneered or frowned.

The new Liberty's building, that apparent ghost from the sixteenth century, was in fact only about ten years old. May climbed the wide wooden stairs to Furnishing and Furnishing Fabrics. As usual, she admired the Knole sofas, so casually held together by their tasselled ropes. She would have a plain coloured one, with round silk damask cushions to offset the squareness. She tried to imagine herself sitting on one with Tom Crosby, but he would probably look just as uncomfortable at the offer as Detective Sergeant Price had done. She felt a little guilty about not having contacted Price. Then again, she could just imagine his response if she called up to mention the shooting of Rex Braddon: 'We know all about that, thank you very much, miss.' She seemed destined to investigate alone, and that was what differentiated her from all the complacent shoppers in Liberty's, most of them as plush and highly coloured as the goods they were buying.

At the bottom of Regent Street the stone arch brought her out on another cavalcade: Piccadilly. She was just thinking she ought to buy a present for her father as she was passing Hatchard's, more or less officially the smartest bookshop in Britain. Her father read a good deal, which was probably the reason she did. She received a rather formal greeting from the young man at the counter, as if this were a hotel rather than a bookshop, and climbed the stairs, thickly carpeted in green and gold, to Travel, which of course included Yorkshire as well as Africa.

A Tour of the West Riding by someone other than J. B. Priestley (for once) had a picture of a tram on the cover, so that was out, because of the 'smash' that had nearly killed her dad. She padded on up to Fiction. Dad read Americans: Jack London, Steinbeck, Hemingway. May had read that Hemingway got his stripped-down style from Dashiell Hammett, not the other way around, so she drifted over to crime fiction. But you didn't lightly buy any book with a revolver on the cover for a man who'd spent four years shooting at people and being shot at, then politely changing the subject if you brought it up. But *The Thin Man* by Hammett was available as a green Penguin. She read it for a while, finding a certain northern-ness in the tone, oddly enough, and bought it, together with another Maugham novel for herself – *Ashenden*, about a secret agent in the War. She paid an extra sixpence for the man at the front counter to wrap *The Thin Man* in green and gold paper with fascinating, machine-like movements before he added the final grace note: a gold ribbon embroidered with the word 'Hatchard's'.

Time for dinner, or 'luncheon' as they called it in Piccadilly. Her staple choices for 'eating out' were ABCs or Lyons, and this was a day to go one better than the Aerated Bread Company, so a Lyons Corner House it must be, and there was one coming up, just before the 'Circus'. But before the white and gold façade of the Lyons was another exotic premises: J&B Tobacconist, its window colourfully crammed with cigarette packets. The interior was dark and hot, with cigarettes and cigars displayed in opened boxes, all in a soft semi-darkness, glass light boxes propped on shelves glowing yellow with the names of the brands on the front. She saw only the familiar Player's, Capstan, Bristol and so on.

The man behind the counter was holding his cigarette elegantly between long fingers, as though demonstrating how it should be done. 'Good afternoon, madam,' he said, suavely. In an alcove behind him, half hidden by a curtain, was a man reading a newspaper and looking surly.

'Do you have the Star brand?' May asked.

'Twenties?'

'Yes.'

The man frowned, as if May had called his bluff. He was forced to relinquish some of his dignity as he ferreted under the counter for a while. Eventually he emerged. 'Sorry, miss, looks like we're just out. Not a lot of call for Stars. They're quite strong,' he added. 'Not usually a lady's smoke.'

'I was hoping to buy some for a friend,' May said, thinking that this 'friend' would only have received them if he deigned to get in touch *and* proved conclusively that he had not shot Rex Braddon.

'*Star* man?' said the tobacconist. 'We probably know him.' By 'we' he must mean himself and the unsavoury man in the alcove.

'He's called Tom Crosby,' said May and, since there was no sign of recognition, she added, 'he has a slight American accent.'

'Not ringing any bells,' said the tobacconist.

As May stepped out of the shop she heard the man in the alcove say, 'You do know him, Mike. Nervy sort of chap – always seems a bit on edge.'

She saw herself reflected in a long mirror on which the words 'Piccadilly Tens' descended diagonally. She looked small and pale, like an urchin, alone in the big world – far more like someone who would *be* murdered than someone who would solve a murder. She walked on to the Lyon's, but her appetite had fled.

May was shown to a table where an early edition of the *Evening News* had been left. The headline (HITLER 'LOSING PATIENCE') did nothing to settle her nerves. She pushed it aside as the Nippy came up. May ordered fish pie. As she waited for it to arrive she read the opening of *Ashende*n, but it wasn't very distracting. He was a very easy-going secret agent, who took almost as many hot baths as May did. Surely Maugham's style was too leisurely, but he must be doing something right. The fish pie fortified her to face the *Evening News*, the inside pages at least. On page five she read:

ENGINE DRIVER FOUND

Mr Dougal Byrne, 62, reported missing from the vicinity of King's Cross station by his employers, the London & North Eastern Railway, has been found safe and well by police in Edinburgh. A spokesman expressed the gratefulness of Scotland Yard to all who assisted in the search.

As usual with those kinds of stories, the reader was left to their own morbid speculations. It would not do to state in cold print that Mr Byrne had gone mad. In any event, he had not been murdered, and so, in the absence of any new moquette-related outrage, the focus was back on the murder of Rex Braddon, and therefore also on Tom Crosby. May's anxiety returned. She could not face pudding.

6

Westminster Bridge Road was a 'principal thoroughfare', so May found it on her Tube map: a long road of old offices and warehouses, mostly closed at this time on a summer's evening. Yet here, at number 61, was this artistic centre, new and modern Morley College.

In the sparse lobby May read the list of departments: Print Making and Bookbinding; Library, Lecture Studio, Refectory . . . A nearby door of wood and frosted glass was half-open. May heard a confident, upper-class female voice. 'Don't look at hers, Molly, darling,' the voice was saying, and then, 'Light *does* come into it with charcoal, you know, Duncan.'

Just inside the door was a notice on an easel, as if it were a small work of art itself. It read 'Life Class. Tutor, Mrs Nancy Marshall.' The artists worked in a circle around the model, some in pencil, some in charcoal. Despite the half-open door the room was hot and stuffy, presumably for the benefit of the model, who wore a sheet that covered (apparently accidentally) his privates. He was fat, florid and bald, except for some wisps of grey hair combed forward. If you thought of the bedsheet as a toga, he looked like Nero. It was hard to imagine what might have motivated him to sit as a model. Perhaps he was immune to unflattering depictions of himself. Perhaps he never looked at the depictions, but he couldn't help hearing the remarks of the tutor, Mrs Marshall. 'Look at the lumps on the forehead,' she was advising someone, but the model didn't appear to mind. He seemed both pleased with his near-nakedness and rather prim; he kept readjusting his toga.

Mrs Marshall had an angular pale face with large blue eyes; her hair was retained in an untidy bob by a rather thick red pencil with gold lettering running along it. She held another pencil of the same make in her hand. She wore a well-cut suit of grey flannel; there was some dried mud on her boots and this, along the slight pinkness in her cheeks ('wind-burned' might be the phrase), put May in mind of an outdoor Virginia Woolf. She walked around the circle as relentlessly as the hand of a clock, commenting on her students' efforts, and there was Ellie, at twelve o'clock, on the opposite side of the room from May. The sight of Ellie was always cheering. She smiled and held up a hand to indicate five minutes. Then she mimicked drinking a cup of tea. She meant for May to wait in the refectory, but May was hypnotised by Mrs Marshall, who, if she had noticed May (and she must have, since she obviously noticed everything), did not seem to mind her presence.

Clearly Mrs Marshall was in her element. She had now removed the pencil from the hand of a grey-haired man and was drawing on his sketch pad with her own pencil. 'You're a doctor, Stafford, darling, so you're too anatomical. Be freer in your interpretation of the human body.'

'Easier said than done,' he said.

'Then have a pint of beer before the next class, Stafford. Have two! And please buy a new pencil.' She snapped the man's pencil in half and gave him the one from the back of her hair, which caused her hair to fall down. 'A soft one like this, Stafford, not that scalpel of yours!'

'Thanks,' the man said, looking at the new pencil. 'I promise I'll give you it back at the end of the class.'

It was a gracious offer in the circumstances, but Mrs Marshall merely laughed, shaking her head. She was already on to the next student in the circle, a rather faded middle-aged lady, who seemed braced for an assault. Nancy Marshall looked at her work, and made no remark, which was ominous. She then looked at the work of the clerkly man in the next seat. Then she began very pointedly looking from the one to the other in turn.

'Suspiciously similar,' she said at length. 'Have you two been drawing each other's drawings? How many times have I told you? Look with your own eyes!'

The faded woman looked quite upset. Mrs Marshall leaned towards her and whispered in her ear. Then she kissed her on the cheek. 'Don't mind me, darling Penny! Your drawing of Mr Forsyth's drawing is technically excellent. But if you must copy, go to the National Gallery!'

As May turned back towards the door Mrs Marshall was saying to the next student, 'Where's the light coming from, John? I can't tell, from this.' Even when May was halfway across the lobby she heard, 'Look at Eleanor's, John. She has an idea and she's following it through. It's a slightly *strange* idea, but I rather like it.'

By 'Eleanor', Mrs Marshall meant 'Ellie', and May was pleased for her friend, especially when she remembered how

55

Ellie had ended up in dilapidated Islington and how Anthony Johnson was messing her about. But there was also a twinge of jealousy, in light of May's latest rejection slip, and this was a familiar feeling. Ever since their days at Princess Mary's High School, May had suspected that Ellie would become a professional artist before she herself became a professional writer.

The refectory was a basic (and largely empty) café, but the walls were covered in paintings – a mural, in fact, and it was rather overwhelming, like seeing a heavily tattooed man. There appeared to be fairy-tale scenes, some of which gradually resolved into Shakespearean. May saw Caliban and Romeo and Juliet, but she was not as familiar with Shakespeare as she ought to be. Wherever possible, it seemed, the women were naked. What she liked best was a depiction of a large doll's house, its inhabitants dreamily independent of one another. The rooms were mainly red or pink; the sky was grey with yellow clouds, so it was hard to tell the time of day.

Ellie arrived in the canteen – *flowed* in, you might say, in her long green frock and longish blue, silky coat. Blue and green, it was said, were 'never to be seen', but they were if you had the right blue and green, which Ellie obviously did. She was holding her satchel-like handbag.

'It's by Eric Ravilious and Edward Bawden,' she said, indicating the mural. 'I think mainly Ravilious. He does lovely countryside scenes in watercolour, and he's a really excellent designer. Not very good at people, though. If you look at that woman walking up the stairs, she's slightly plodding, don't you think? And that's his wife, so she shouldn't be plodding. What shall we get to eat?'

May had a cheese salad, Ellie the chicken pie and chipped potatoes she'd spoken of in her letter.

'Let's have a look, then,' said May, indicating Ellie's sketch pad as they sat down.

Ellie had sketched, in smudgy charcoal, only the nose and the left eye of the model, which looked both highly grotesque and accurate. 'I was thinking vaguely of Goya,' she said. 'I was trying to get across the whole of the person via that little bit of his face.'

'Well, I think you succeeded, love. And the teacher obviously liked it.'

'Yes, well. She did today.' But Ellie was clearly pleased.

They started to eat, Ellie as usual at twice the speed of May.

May said, 'She seems quite ferocious, though.'

'Mrs Marshall? I like her. I like her because she reminds me of me.'

'How do you mean?' asked May, although she did know.

'No-nonsense. Can you imagine how anyone can end up so direct without being from Yorkshire?'

'Where *is* she from?'

'Don't know. The south. She's pretty grand. She was married to a famous painter: Bernard Marshall.'

'Never heard of him.'

'He was a famous painter nonetheless, dear.'

'So he's dead?'

'But getting more famous all the time. Do you want pudding?'

'No. Well, maybe an apple.'

'For God's sake. I'm going to have apple pie.'

But she made no move to get it. Pushing her plate aside, Ellie leaned forward. 'Something's happened, hasn't it? Something or some*one*.'

'I did meet quite an interesting man on Saturday.'

'You mean a good-looking man?'

'Yes, but also interesting.'

And May began talking about Tom as if she harboured no suspicions about him. She knew perfectly well this was reprehensible boasting, but it was also an experiment: to see whether she could convince herself of his innocence.

'He's a journalist – a special correspondent.'

'So far so good.'

'On a railway magazine.'

'Oh.'

'Why "Oh"?'

'You know why. Because railways are boring.'

'He likes trains. But he loves journalism more.'

'Well, thank God for that.'

'He's very ambitious, I think.'

'We're all ambitious, love.'

'And he's American.'

'We're back on track! Does he call women "dames"?'

'No.'

'Does he call a "jumper" a "sweater"?'

'That hasn't come up.'

'Does he say "sure" instead of "yes"?'

'I think he did once.'

'Well, how did you meet him?'

'Because of this,' said May, taking the moquette from her bag.

'A bit of material,' said Ellie, reaching across the table for it. 'What is it? Moquette?'

She knows that because she's a Halifax girl, thought May.

'Nice pattern,' said Ellie, handing it back. 'Explain.'

When May had finished Ellie said, 'Just a minute. Rex Braddon, did you say?'

May nodded.

'Wait here a minute,' said Ellie, and she went off somewhere.

A couple of minutes later she came back. 'There's an exhibition of Braddon's work, and tonight it's the opening thingy, the private view. Some people in the class were talking about it. Mrs Marshall's just off, but she said—'

'Hold on,' said May. 'She's just off to the exhibition?'

'No. Off home. Evidently she doesn't think Braddon's work is up to much, but she knows the gallery owner, and she said to say her name and he'd let us in. It's the West Gallery in Bond Street. But we'll have to get a move on.' Ellie hadn't sat down since returning.

May stood up. 'But Rex Braddon's dead,' she reminded Ellie.

'The exhibition was arranged before he died. It was going to be a retrospective – you know, a survey of his life's work – and that's still what it is, only with a big full stop because, obviously he won't be producing any more work.'

'There was nothing about it in the newspaper.'

'I think they were going to cancel it, but now it's going ahead as a kind of tribute to him, I suppose. There'll be champagne.'

*

They took the Northern Line up to Tottenham Court Road.

On the train, another red one, Ellie asked for another look at the moquette. 'The black and yellow's unusual,' she said. 'Slightly Japanese, I reckon.'

'Are you saying it's by a Japanese designer?'

'Obviously not. But Japanese art was quite a big thing twenty years ago, so maybe it's by an old designer, and maybe a woman too.'

'Why?'

'The flower – and women do tend to do moquette. Like this one we're sitting on.'

It was the amusingly regimented leaf design.

'It's by Marion Dorn,' said Ellie. 'She's the most wonderful designer. Scarves, throws, curtains, carpets. She's American. When she was a girl she had TB and spent all her time lying in bed thinking about colour and form. It makes me quite jealous that she was so ill. You can see her carpets in Claridge's. We should go there for a small sherry, love, and it would *have* to be a small one with their prices. She might be there tonight.'

'At Claridge's?'

'At the party, you daft 'aporth. It's going to be quite a big "do". You could ask her about this,' she said, handing the moquette back. 'She lives with Eddie Kauffer.'

'Who's he?'

'Edward McKnight Kauffer. He's a brilliant poster artist.'

'He'd have to be with a name like that.'

'You'll have seen his stuff in Tube stations. It's extreme: Cubist, Expressionist. He makes even lettering look sort of industrial. Words coming at the end of girders or pipes, and things look disjointed, like a collage, because obviously things *are* disjointed, especially in London. But he can also be surreal. You must have seen that lovely, dreamy one of an ordinary-looking suburban couple and their little girl – all three of them floating off through the sky to catch a country bus from some station you can reach by the Underground. The man's smoking a pipe and wearing a homburg hat, but he has angel's wings. They all do, and it's all pinks, browns and powder blues.'

Other conversation in the carriage had fallen silent; everyone was listening to this tall, loud, beautiful girl from the North.

'Marion Dorn met Eddie Kauffer in Paris, and they ran away together. They have a flat in Chelsea. Evidently it's lovely – full of Modernist furniture.'

Here Ellie fell silent, perhaps thinking of her own bedsit. May had not yet seen it; Ellie said she would invite her when it was 'ready', but May suspected that even now it would already be more strikingly done out than her own place. Ellie's art would be all over the walls, just as it had been in her Halifax bedroom. She had apparently also bought a couple of Underground posters from a London Transport shop in one of the central London Tube stations – May couldn't recall which one. The posters were 'originals' in some sense and surprisingly cheap – about five bob – and Ellie had cut off the bit at the bottom that gave the boring information about train times.

The train had stopped in the tunnel.

'Tell me more about your new boy,' Ellie said, and the whole carriage looked towards May for her response, or so it seemed to May.

'He's not mine and he's not a boy,' she said, in a much quieter tone than her friend's. 'He's probably about twenty-three – and he's quite shy, which can be charming.'

'How is he shy? Does he keep going red?'

'No. He never goes red, but he doesn't always look at you . . . But then again you don't want a man who stares into your eyes all the time.'

The train was moving again.

'But you do want one who looks at you occasionally,' said Ellie. 'Just to make sure you're still *there*, and so on. Are you sure he hasn't got something to hide?'

May knew what was coming next and she was braced for it.

'May,' said Ellie, 'are you sure *he* didn't kill Braddon?'

'Don't be so daft.' But of course, she wasn't quite sure.

'Well, why was he hanging about outside the flat?'

'I've told you: because he knew Braddon. He'd interviewed him.' May had skipped over the detail of the copy approval business. 'You're just being provocative,' May said.

'Someone's got to provoke you, love,' said Ellie. 'You wouldn't be here in London were it not for me.'

That was her familiar line, but it wasn't true. Ellie had talked non-stop about the Exchange ever since they'd started at Quarmby's as seventeen-year-olds, but May was always going to do it.

'You're wrong,' said May.

'I hope I am,' said Ellie, and on that uncomfortable note they remained silent as the train hurtled from Leicester Square to Tottenham Court Road.

They were back talking on the Central Line train, though (whose moquette was an uneventful green and brown check).

'What's this magazine he works on again?' said Ellie.

May took the *Railway Digest* from her bag. 'He says his boss, the editor, doesn't have a proper understanding of what people want to read.'

Ellie flicked through the pages. 'He certainly doesn't have a proper understanding of what *I* want to read. But the office is in London EC.' She was pointing to the page where the magazine's address, Whitefriars Street, appeared. 'So it's not *totally* obscure. And he's got to start somewhere.'

May was grateful for this conciliation, but on the whole she wanted to stop thinking about Tom. It was too exhausting.

7

There was quite a crowd outside the West Gallery. 'Oh, look,' said Ellie. 'I think that's Marion Dorn – that lady standing half on the pavement, half on the road . . . No, I don't think it is.' She touched May on the arm to indicate the jeweller's window they were passing. Turning to her reflection in it, Ellie began applying eye black, passing her lipstick to May. 'Just in case you do meet a man who *does* look at you,' she said.

A decorative young woman in black had the guest list. Her clothes suggested she was in mourning for the dead artist; her wide smile suggested she was not.

'You'll not find us on there, love,' said Ellie, in broad Yorkshire, and when May saw the girl's smile falter she thought she'd better intervene.

'Mrs Marshall – Nancy, at the Morley College – said to mention her name.'

The smile returned. 'That's fine,' said the decorative woman. 'Is Mrs Marshall coming?'

'Not sure about that,' said May.

'No,' Ellie said to the woman. 'She's not.'

'If you'd like to sign the book,' said the woman.

It was a wide ledger, strategically placed on the way to the drinks table. There was space for 'Name', 'Address' and a space beyond, in which some people had attempted to formulate commiserations or commendations of the artist. May and Ellie left it blank, as had most other people. The pen they had found in the well of the book contained purple ink, and so all the entries and remarks were in purple – the colour of the signature on the note sent to Scotland Yard with the moquette. May couldn't remember whether she'd mentioned the purple ink to Ellie.

'Now drinks,' Ellie said.

A good many of the champagne flutes on the table had already toppled over. Fortunately the bottles – attended by a decorative young man – were all still upright. He poured their glasses to the brim, while saying to an elegant woman about twice his age who wore her hair in a very chic, albeit old-fashioned, Eton crop, 'I absolutely *would* buy figs just for their colour. Pomegranates too.'

Ellie clinked her glass against May's, which seemed rather disrespectful of the deceased. Then again, nobody seemed to be talking about Rex Braddon. A scruffy but posh man next to May was saying, 'You should *know* that it's more expensive to send a telegram at night.'

'It's vintage,' said Ellie, who'd already drunk half her glass.

'Can you tell by the taste?'

'I can tell by the label on the bottles.' Ellie looked towards the heart of the throng. 'It's a bit of all right, this,' she said. 'I'd like to draw *him*,' she added, looking in the direction of a tousle-haired man who was quite good-looking despite having a somewhat wolfishly projecting nose. 'Will you excuse me, love?' she said to May. 'I'm off to see if there's anybody from the RCA.' The Royal College of Art: Ellie wanted to go there on a scholarship.

On a table near the visitors' a sort of shrine to Braddon had been created. A photograph, propped up, showed an imperious, leonine man with flowing hair and beard. Other photographs showed the artist in what looked a series of fancy dress costumes: wide brimmed hats, a cloak retained at the neck by a chain, velvety-looking jodhpurs. Sometimes he was photographed alongside other people, but he was never really 'with' them.

A large encyclopaedia of art was open at the page that featured Braddon. The entry was of above average length by the standards of the book, but bland and non-committal, relying mainly on lists. Braddon was a 'painter in oils and watercolour, a print maker, draughtsman, sculptor and a creator of applied art.' His works had been compared to those of . . . almost everybody, it seemed. He'd been born in Chelsea, the son of a barrister, saw action throughout the war, attended the Royal College of Art briefly. 'Likely to be considered his most interesting work is a series of landscapes of the early 1920s, uncharacteristic of his subsequent output and which he called his "dream sequence".' He had become a Fellow of the Royal Academy in 1937 – this must be a new book, therefore, or a new edition, at least. The same photograph as the one propped-up on the table was also in this book, as was a single example of Braddon's work: a portrait of a pretty, smug-looking woman. 'Mrs Diana Sutton', it was captioned.

May was reminded that this was an art exhibition. You ought to look at 'the work' in return for your drink. She fought her way through to a framed poster, or at least the painting from which a poster had been made. It showed a starry sky, with a train diagonally crossing a full moon – an advertisement for the Night Ferry, which May had vaguely heard of. It was a train operating in conjunction with a boat in some way she didn't understand. It took you to France, anyhow.

'Of course, that was to commission,' someone was saying, 'but a lot of his paintings were posterised later, I suppose because they had obvious commercial appeal – nostalgic, sentimental or whatever.'

The speaker was definitely not in mourning, his suit being the same powder blue as the sky in the poster, his tie bright red. His female companion was also flamboyant in blue, so they had a dress sense in common, as well as a certain flatness of tone when it came to discussing Rex Braddon.

'Is there a catalogue?' said the woman.

'I think we're all going to be sent one,' said the man. 'They had to re-do it at the last minute.'

'Why so?'

'Well, after the . . . They had to put it all in the past tense, I suppose.'

'He was mainly . . . landscapes, wasn't he?'

'Did all sorts – lot of portraits. Society people, you know.'

A landscape was next to the train poster: hilly fields in a washed-out green, offset by a quaint red tractor in the foreground.

'A bit Ravilious?' said the woman.

'Don't tell Eric that, whatever you do.'

'Paul Nash?'

'Not as melancholic. Not as profound. His best things are some early landscapes. *There's* one.' In the chink between the heads of gossiping people was a smaller painting. It showed a farmhouse – and whole farm, indeed – set among trees and whirled in a green and red circle. 'Called those his "dreams",' said the man in powder blue. 'They constitute about one per cent of his output, or less. So that's the extent to which he was interesting.'

May realised she was hearing what the compiler of the encyclopaedia had not dared write.

The man, seeing that May had overheard his negative re-marks, did have the grace to blush slightly. 'Braddon was in the army with Paul, I think,' he said, addressing his compan-ion but continuing to look at May. 'Well, he was in the army with a lot of people, given that he was in France throughout the whole show. That was his natural milieu, I can't help thinking: war.'

May could hear Ellie's too-loud voice talking about Halifax – about Quarmby's, in fact. 'You've heard of the Harrod's of the North?' she was saying. 'Well, that's not Quarmby's.'

'Is Paul *here*?' the woman was saying to the man.

'Haven't seen him.'

'Any of the women?'

The man shrugged and sighed. 'There were so *many,*' he said. He was now smiling quite broadly at May. Perhaps she ought to capitalise by asking about Braddon's involvement, if any, with moquette?

But it seemed somebody was about to make a speech. A head had appeared above the crowd. It was a sleek, largely bald head, above a well-filled velvet jacket. The man resembled an expensive cushion in human form. As he began (and his voice wasn't quite loud enough for May to hear every word), Ellie returned to May's side. 'That's Mr West,' she said, 'Aubrey West – the gallerist.'

Was he the provider of the purple ink, wondered May?

West was thanking everyone for coming. This was both a deeply sad occasion and an opportunity to celebrate the life and work of a great artist. He had agonised about whether to continue with the exhibition, which had been months in the planning. When the terrible news came through he had been minded to call it off, but Rex Braddon's agent (Madeleine somebody or other) had strongly encouraged him to go ahead.

'Well, she would do?' Ellie whispered, half to herself and half to May – and Ellie's whispers were not very quiet. She must have been overheard, but there had been other, similarly irreverent mutterings.

The last word, West was saying, had been with Rex Braddon's sister (his next of kin, in the absence of any wife or children, it appeared), and she had given her consent to what had now become a tribute and memorial to her brother. (West was indicating somebody in the crowd: the woman with the Eton crop.) 'Rex Braddon . . . Doesn't the photograph on the table say it all?' Further mutterings here, and it was as though West wanted to elicit them. 'A military bearing,' he said, 'seemed the operative phrase.'

Braddon, he continued, could be 'intimidating and peremptory, but on the other hand—' The credit side of the equation was inaudible to May, however. He remained 'in essence a soldier,' said West, who now embarked on a joke:

'Whereas to most people in this room, the Ypres Salient might be a characteristic brush stroke of some Belgian modernist, to Major Rex Braddon it was an all-too real place – and not a very nice one either.'

His biography came through in fragments. Although essentially self-taught, he had 'looked in' on the Royal College of Art briefly after the army. He had been on the 'Design' course there, along with . . . and here West optimistically pronounced three or four names, like a schoolmaster taking the register, but there was no answering response from the room, only the continuing undercurrent of treachery.

Had somebody in this room shot Braddon, May wondered? On the whole, those present looked too well-off to be murderers; too much to lose and not enough to gain. There was one slightly desperate-looking man, May had noticed. He was small but tough-looking, like a jockey. He wore a cheap, grey suit and he'd been drunkenly asking somebody for a cigarette. She couldn't see him just now. Perhaps he had left, although she doubted that. He would remain as long as the vintage champagne did.

It was the champagne that had drawn this crowd, May believed, not the character of the deceased man – and the morbid fascination that Tom had admitted to might also have played a part.

Aubrey West was describing Braddon's career, his 'work'. He was, West suggested, fortunate to have started out at a time of increasing demand for graphic art, from the railways especially. In the early days that had funded his less commercial work, until his reputation as a fine portraitist and painter of landscapes grew. But the phrase 'Jack of all trades' hung unspoken in the air, which was increasingly smoky, with more and more people lighting cigarettes, as though in protest at the speech. Ellie had drifted away again; May couldn't see her.

'Did he get the recognition he deserved?' West had just asked, rhetorically, and the room seemed to freeze. It seemed to May that everybody was waiting, as the blue smoke twisted slowly over their heads.

'He got what he deserved in the end,' an upper-class male voice said, very clearly.

There were mutterings of protest. A similar voice from the crowd said, equally loudly, 'Shame on you, Guy.'

West was stooping, conferring quite calmly with someone. It was as though he had anticipated this outburst but was nonetheless seeking reassurance about his next move. He was nodding as he received counsel from the other person. He stood upright again. 'Guy,' he said. 'That remark does you no credit. I don't think for one minute that you really believe it, but I'm going to have to ask you to leave. Guy, please leave.'

But the man didn't need to be asked twice. He was making a rather dignified and formal exit. People stood aside for him as he made for the door. May pushed through the crowd to observe his departure. The man was tall and thin, with a halo of curly white hair, onto which he pressed a crumpled Panama as he stepped through the door.

He immediately hailed a taxi, and if it had pulled up for him his exit would have been perfect, but the taxi didn't stop. Nor did the man, though. He was stalking away in the direction of the Tube station, with May walking fast after him, while removing the moquette from her bag. Another

71

taxi was coming up – there was a limitless supply of them in Bond Street. It stopped for the man, who was 20 yards ahead of May. She began to run; she reached the cab just as it was pulling away, knocking on the rear window and holding up the moquette – waving it as though it were a flag, or something he had forgotten. His eyes did widen when he saw the moquette, but the taxi took him away fast.

8

Ellie was waiting outside the gallery, shielding her eyes against the low sun as she watched May return from her failed mission. Also watching her return, from behind Ellie, was the jockey-like man, who was raising his glass and drinking with a very deliberate motion, suggesting an attempt to control drunkenness.

'Who *was* that?' May asked Ellie, pointing after the taxi. After all, Ellie seemed to know art people, if only by reputation.

'Don't know, but my friend will,' Ellie said, turning her head towards the gallery. 'She knows everybody.'

'He reacted when he saw the moquette,' said May. 'I'm sure it meant something to him.'

'But not enough to stop the cab.'

'Maybe he didn't want to let on that it meant anything to him.'

Ellie's 'friend' was waiting just inside the door. She wore a red headscarf with a white flower print, a loose and low white blouse and grey baggy trousers, which turned out, when you looked further down, to be pantaloons. Ellie did not know this woman from Selfridges, that was obvious enough; she was a bohemian.

'This is Lucy,' said Ellie. 'Lucy Palmer. She sometimes takes the drawing class at Morley when Nancy's off. She's a brilliant artist.'

'Not quite so brilliant as some of my pupils,' said Lucy Palmer.

'Who was that man who's just left?' May asked her.

'He's called Guy Cavanagh,' said Lucy Palmer, who spoke very correctly, like all bohemians. 'He teaches drawing at the Ruskin School of Art.'

'That's in Oxford,' said Ellie.

Lucy Palmer said, 'Ellie's told me about a piece of moquette you've come by. Might I have a look?'

May couldn't really blame Ellie for telling Lucy about the moquette. She had made it clear that she was seeking information about it. But she felt uneasy as she took it out of the bag again, in the middle of that jostling crowd, which seemed to have been galvanised by Guy Cavanagh's outburst. Had it been cathartic? He had said what most people present had been thinking – even the gallerist, Aubrey West, who had finished his speech either at the moment of Cavanagh's interjection or while May had been chasing Cavanagh. May could see West happily drinking champagne and holding court near the drinks table.

Lucy was studying the moquette. 'A policeman brought this to you with a note about a murder?'

May nodded. Lucy wasn't loud like Ellie, but she hadn't liked the way the word 'policeman' had seemed to leap out of her mouth.

'So it's like a sort of magic carpet ride you've been given.'

The small drunk was looking on, too close. He didn't believe in magic carpets.

'I think Enid might approve,' Lucy said. 'A simple pattern but striking. I like the yellow and black. It looks good on bees, so why not on moquette? I'm so sorry,' she said to May. 'Have you heard of Enid Marx? I know Ellie has. Enid's a friend of mine. She's been designing moquette for Frank Pick – for the new trains.'

'Who's Frank Pick?' May asked.

'He's the sort of design chief of London Transport, although you wouldn't know it to meet him.'

'Why not?'

'He comes over as a northern lawyer – which is what he used to be.'

'Northern,' said Ellie. 'That's good.'

'Do you think this is one of his?' said May. 'One for the new trains, I mean?'

'I don't think so. The colours are wrong.'

'Do you think Rex Braddon ever designed moquette?'

'Well, he did a bit of everything, so I wouldn't rule it out, but I'm pretty sure he wasn't in with Edith's lot – the designers for the new trains. He might have been approached. Frank tried to get Paul Nash, but I don't think Paul ever did anything, or maybe he did one that didn't make it onto the trains for some reason. You'd have to ask Frank. It'd be a question of making an appointment.'

'Is he an approachable sort of person?'

'Are northern lawyers approachable? They are if you've sent them a letter explaining in detail why you want to

75

take up their time and they think you've made a good case.'

The young man who'd been behind the drinks table was now at large, dispensing champagne. He refilled Lucy and Ellie's glasses and brought a new one for May. The drinking in the room had generally redoubled since the end of the speech.

May said, 'Perhaps Enid Marx would know who made this?'

'Maybe,' said Lucy. 'She lives on the Finchley Road most of the time, but she's in Scotland just now. Margaret teaches up there. That's her friend, Margaret Lambert.'

'They're lesbians, aren't they?' said Ellie.

'Ellie!' said May, but Lucy didn't seem to mind. She had taken refuge in a sort of wondering smile.

'Which moquettes did Enid do?' asked Ellie. 'Could you describe one of them anyway?

'Enid did some red diamonds on green and black squares. That's one she thought came out best.'

'I haven't seen that one yet,' said May, who realised she was talking about Tube seat coverings as though they were new films on release. 'What does Guy Cavanagh have against Rex Braddon?'

'Probably what a lot of people in this room have against him. Rex was a cad, and as versatile in his caddishness as he was in his art, except that he was better at being a cad than he was at being an artist.'

'Explain,' said Ellie.

'Oh, he talked about people's work in a way meant to undermine them, which is not just a matter of being rude, although he was that as well. He manipulated people, broke promises, primed critics to denounce his rivals, stole ideas, stole wives and girlfriends and was generally an absolutely adorable man!'

'Did he do any of those things to Guy Cavanagh?'

'Well, Guy's confidence is pretty rock-solid; he's not exactly a lady's man, and I shouldn't imagine he's an easy touch for a loan, so perhaps Braddon stole one of his ideas? Guy mainly teaches, but he does have an imagination. He paints a bit, dabbles in design, fabric prints, book jackets and endpapers, and so on.'

Ellie said, 'Do you think he shot Braddon, then?'

May didn't even bother pulling a disapproving face. She'd been trying to think of a diplomatic way of couching the same question, and she was doubly glad Ellie had asked it, since it suggested she might not really think that Tom Crosby had killed Braddon after all.

'I hardly think so,' said Lucy, in that phlegmatic way of hers, which seemed at odds with her flamboyant outfit. 'I mean, Guy was a conchie in the war . . . sorry, one shouldn't use that term. A conscientious objector – so it would be pretty ironic, wouldn't it? If he shot someone, I mean?'

'I'd like to talk to him,' said May.

'That might prove tricky. Bit stand-offish is Guy.'

'A snob, you mean?' said Ellie.

Lucy laughed. 'Might I counter with "formal" and "reserved"? I'm sorry, ladies, but I'm being summoned.'

Well, she knew everybody, after all. The jockey-like man was still looking towards May, Ellie and Lucy.

May wanted to retain the civilised presence of Lucy for as long as possible. 'It was so nice to meet you.' This usually slowed down any London departure, since the other person had to say something polite in reply.

Lucy handed the moquette back. 'When Enid gets back, I'll ask her about this.'

'Please do,' said May. 'You'll remember the pattern, will you?'

'I've taken a mental photograph of it,' said Lucy. 'A colour one.'

As she moved away May checked her again. 'Do you happen to know who that is?' She nudged her glass in the direction of the jockey-like man as discreetly as she could.

'That's Kenneth Cooper, the painter. He's what you might call a semi-primitive – in art and life.'

'Name rings a bell,' said Ellie. 'I think Mrs Marshall mentioned him in the class once. She said he was on her list of the genuinely worthwhile painters in Britain. Or something like that.'

'Cooper has his advocates,' said Lucy. 'I don't remember Nancy saying anything, but she might be a fan. She likes to look beyond the big names; she might have found energy in his work. She might think that he "sees with his own eyes". That's the holy grail for Nancy.'

'Did he know Rex Braddon?'

'I think they were in the army together, possibly? I think Rex might actually have *helped* Ken Cooper at some point. He wasn't a *total* cad, you know. Well, he was really, but he knew he was, which is possibly redeeming, wouldn't you say? He crops up in a novel. It's pretty obscure – by a woman, of course. Autobiographical. The names have been changed, not much else. I just can't remember *her* name.'

'But do you know the title?'

Lucy was looking up to the ceiling, as though communing with a higher force. 'It'll come to me in a minute . . . It's in French . . .'

'The book?' said May, alarmed, because that would be a test indeed of the French imparted to her by various pretty and often tearful Mademoiselles who had come and gone from Princess Mary's like so many butterflies.

'The title,' said Lucy. '*Impasse* – that's it. Must go, dears!' And she was claimed by her fellow bohemians.

'Interesting about Enid Marx,' said Ellie.

'She was interesting about everything.'

'I sometimes wish *I* was a lesbian,' said Ellie, no doubt thinking of the elusive Anthony Johnson.

'Maybe you'll have a holiday romance in Scarborough?'

'Come off it. With the folks hanging around?' Ellie was looking around. 'I'll give it one more go,' she said.

May went over to the display about Braddon and flicked through the art book to the entries under 'C'. There was an entry – a short one – for Kenneth Cooper. He was described as a '"naïve" painter of brooding landscapes and townscapes, in which human figures seldom appear. He has, however, painted a series of portraits of his wife.' May had lost sight of Kenneth Cooper, but given his demeanour she thought he was lucky to have a wife. One of his works was shown in the book: a painting of a village viewed from a distance. The houses looked as though made from a child's building bricks. Presumably the force of the painting was in the colours, not disclosed on the black and white page.

Then she looked under 'P' and found an entry – also small – for Lucy Palmer. She had been trained at the Slade School of Fine Art. Despite teaching drawing she was 'chiefly known as an engraver and printmaker', depicting scenes of 'psychological conflict'. The example given was a woodcut (May thought that was the term) showing a couple on a seaside promenade with large fairy-lights hanging overhead. On the face of it this was a happy scene, but the sea was perhaps becoming rough; the fairy-lights were a little disordered, and the man seemed to be ignoring the woman. Lucy Palmer had seemed very well balanced for a depicter of psychological conflict.

If Lucy Palmer was in the book, perhaps Guy Cavanagh, of the Ruskin School of Art, would be? He was indeed, albeit with another small entry. Cavanagh was an 'artist, draughtsman', a depicter of classical and biblical scenes. He had also dabbled in book design. After Oxford University he had 'undergone training for the Catholic priesthood.'

Had he, then, become a priest? Presumably not, given that he worked as an art teacher, and given his earlier remark about how Braddon deserved to be shot. In fact, Cavanagh must have repented of religion entirely.

Back among the crowd May encountered Ellie.

'It's a dead loss, this,' Ellie said, a reversal of her earlier verdict. But the party had changed. Before, it had been wary; now it was wilder and louder. It was more evident that everybody knew everybody else.

'Did you meet anybody from the RCA?'

'Did I heckers. And what's the point? I couldn't afford to go even if I passed the exam.'

'Don't they have scholarships?' Ellie had often mentioned these.

'They have *travel* scholarships. All right if you want to go to Italy and draw ruins.' Here was one of the worrying things about Ellie. She went from being ebullient to despondent in a second.

'Do you ever think of going back to Halifax?' Ellie said, and it was not the first time she'd asked that question.

'I *am* going back – tomorrow.'

'Sorry, love. Forgot.'

'Perhaps we'll bump into each other at King's Cross? My train's about eight.'

Ellie shook her head. 'Mine's at six.'

And she'll have to take a bus, or walk it with her suitcase, thought May, since Ellie didn't live on a Tube line.

The unpleasant man, Cooper, was right in front of them. He held an empty champagne glass. 'What are you doing with that?' he said, looking at May's Gladstone bag.

May said, 'What do you mean what am I doing with it? It's my bag.'

The man took a rapid step to the side, as if to stop himself falling over. 'What you've got inside it. Something from the police. You're in with the police.'

'Go away,' said Ellie.

'And why you keep . . . looking at me.'

'I do not keep looking at you. I've been trying to avoid looking at you, if you must know.'

The gallerist, Aubrey West, was coming over.

'You can't go round . . . aspersions,' Cooper was saying. 'You've got trouble coming, lady. Big trouble.'

Casting his eyes upwards in apology to May and Ellie, West took Cooper aside, but as he was saying things like 'Kenneth, be reasonable,' it seemed Cooper was not listening, and he was watching Ellie and May as they made for the door.

9

Under a rusty-coloured sky they joined the flow of pedestrians towards Bond Street Tube station. In the ticket hall some flowers for sale had wilted and the air was full of their sickly smell, combined with the elusive Tube smell of dust and hot electricity.

'Tomorrow, love,' said Ellie, as they showed their tickets at the barrier, 'we'll be in Yorkshire, and Kenneth flipping Cooper won't be.'

May couldn't bear to think of Ellie's lonely journey home. But she seemed to have brightened slightly now that she was out of the gallery and in the crowded, colourful Tube. 'Will you be popping into Quarmby's?' Ellie asked.

May had been wondering about this. It would be much simpler not to. She had been back to the store a couple of times since moving to London, and while everyone asked how you were getting on, half of them – the ones in the habit of saying 'London's not for me' – clearly hoped you were regretting your leap in the dark. 'I think I will,' and her sudden decision prompted a further thought. 'Can I take your sketch up with me? I'd like to show it to Mrs Henderson.' Mrs Henderson was the fashion buyer at Quarmby's.

Consequently, Quarmby's fashions were good, even if its furniture and fabrics, haberdashery and homewares were not.

'She's not going to want to see a drawing of a fat, ugly man's nose, is she?' said Ellie, but she was already taking it from her bag. It really was beautifully done, and only grotesque in the sense that the eye and the nose were fully alive.

Mrs Lilian Henderson had been married once but was no longer, and she didn't need a husband. She was what was called 'independently wealthy', inhabiting a large house that was officially a 'Hall' out at Hollywell Green, a short tram ride from Halifax – not that Mrs Henderson used the trams. She seemed to float above Halifax. She had no discernible accent; if she didn't want to wear a hat, she simply didn't. One afternoon May had seen a bottle of what she assumed was very good red wine on Mrs Henderson's desk in her office on the top floor at Quarmby's, which was always filled with flowers and where a fire burned every winter's day.

Instead of husbands Mrs Henderson brazenly had her 'friends' – all men and sometimes almost boys, tending to be in their late twenties or thirties, whereas Mrs Henderson was at least fifty. Every so often, May thought, one or other of them must have been mistaken for her son. She was 'fast' but elegant with it, and May always thought of her as resembling the heroine of *Chéri* by Colette, which was one of those books you were surprised to find in Halifax Library, and would only take out if certain librarians weren't at the issue desk. You'd have thought *Chéri* would be the name of the book's heroine, but that was Léa. Chéri was the wealthy young man who was her lover. Léa was 49, with large blue 'tranquil' eyes with 'thick chestnut lashes', which could also be said of

Mrs Henderson, who did not, however, unlike Léa, have an 'opulent bust', and women who *did* have them tended not to fit comfortably into Mrs Henderson's favoured product lines.

Mrs Henderson was a great supporter of the Exchange – had possibly even initiated it along with Mr Quarmby, but she herself was an argument against taking up the offer. While it was easy to imagine her in London, on some tree-lined street with large white houses, there was no evidence that she'd ever lived there. She didn't need London any more than she needed anything or anyone.

At Tottenham Court Road, May and Ellie kissed and wished each other good luck with their respective trips. As the train pulled away, May lingered on the platform to give a last wave, but Ellie was not waving back. Instead, she was mouthing one word over and over – a word she had evidently forgotten to say when they were together, or that had just occurred to her. While this repeated shout was quite inaudible to May because of the window glass and the train's roar, May had the impression that the passengers were regarding her friend with bemusement. Perhaps it was a northern word Ellie was shouting, or some technical term relating to art and artists? Ellie had twisted around to keep May in view and give her every chance of comprehending. But the train, which was not one of the trim red ones but a primitive-looking purple thing, had now removed itself from the station, leaving a green light in the tunnel, which became a rudely staring red.

May was alone on the platform. A poster on the white wall showed a blurry watercolour cartoon of an elephant and rhinoceros in a cocktail bar. It advertised 'Zoo Nights'. The Zoo was open till 11.30 on Thursdays and Fridays. The sign above May's head, still swinging gently in the train's wake, indicated 'Northern Line' with a very delicate arrow.

This London Tube, thought May, was beautiful and brutal at the same time. Had Ellie been distressed as she shouted? Possibly not, but some important revelation had come to her. Perhaps she would be waiting for May at Holborn. Unlikely: Ellie had to get up very early in the morning, and if it really were a matter of life or death she could always come around to May's place.

When the red train drew in to the Northern Line platform May sought the smoking carriage. *The smokers will protect you.* Tom Crosby was a smoker. In the end, she had been sorry not to see him at the gallery party, simply because he was so nice to look at. There were four other people in the carriage, but May was alone again by Belsize. Though other people besides herself alighted, she found herself alone in the lift; the rest seemed simply to have disappeared. Her nerves were somewhat soothed by the 'Goodnight, Miss', from the man at the barrier, but Rosslyn Hill was too quiet. The three illuminated maps outside the station conveyed their information to nobody. Car headlights were approaching as she crossed the road, but when she turned into Ornan Road a heavy silence reasserted itself. Ornan Road had largely gone to sleep. Only a few lights showed in the big Victorian villas, and those from behind closed curtains.

There were footsteps behind May. Were they the footsteps of a drunken man? Possibly, because they kept starting and stopping. The front gardens were bounded by thick, dark hedges, which blended in with the moonless night. Gardeners had treacherously created niches in these, ostensibly for gates, but it seemed to May that the man behind her was moving from one of these niches to another. She had seen him only from the corner of her eye and dare not turn round. Once she got to Belsize Lane she would be all right. No shops would be open, but some lights might still be on for cashing up, doing the books.

But Belsize Lane also slept. As May took her key from her bag she saw the rolled moquette – certainly now holding the promise of trouble, not adventure. In the stone well she fumbled with the key and the lock, and when she was finally in she closed the door behind her with a bang which, she knew as she stood motionless in the dark room, had been a silly thing to do. She ought to have closed the door quietly.

She realised she had made another mistake in filling out her address in the guest book at the gallery. Or had she simply been followed? Still holding her bag, she sat down on her bed. She ought not to switch on the lights. She could do nothing but listen. After a minute or so of silence she began to think she had imagined the whole thing. She was highly imaginative, after all, as people had been telling her all her life.

There came a new noise – the rattly sound of a London taxi. It was not directly outside her rooms, but not far off – a few doors down. Anybody who knew her address might not be able to make out the house numbers in the dark. Yes, her guess must be right, because now came the other taxi noises – somebody climbing out; the muttering of voices, passenger to driver; then a slight lessening of darkness – the taxi putting its light back on. And now the sound of its departure.

Silence, then approaching bootsteps. What was the

connection between these and the ones she had heard behind her on Ornan Road? The walker would soon be at the top of the steps leading down to the cursed 'area'. Her only further refuge was through the ridiculous bead curtain and into the 'kit-bath'. But at least if she did that she might not be visible to anyone peering through the window. She stood up, but the bootsteps from the street were quieter; the person was walking away, and May found she was shaking, not so much with fear as rage – anger at her own cowardice. She was, in effect, cowering in a hole. She got up and went back to the door.

There was no point just standing in the dark area, if she didn't climb the steps to the street. At first she could see nobody, but as she looked towards Ornan Road she saw a figure: a man walking away, but slowly. Of course she mustn't pursue him. She must settle for the fact that he was departing.

Back indoors she lit a candle and went and sat on her bed again, thinking over what she had seen. The night was dark. The only reason she had been able to make out the man was that his upper half had been pale. Tom Crosby had worn a white jacket on the Saturday when she met him. It was a further hour before she felt able to undress for bed.

10

May went to Halifax in her blue afternoon dress, with her almost exactly matching blue straw hat and the red velvet flower in it. The red brought out the blueness of her eyes, as did the blueness of everything else. Her Gladstone bag carried the moquette and her father's present. As far as she could tell, no strange man followed her to the Tube station. It occurred to her that among her other indiscretions at the private view she had let slip the time of her train to the north. But the only stares at King's Cross were from the usual sources: rivalrous young women, and men in general.

The guard itemised every element of the simmering train alongside them, which seemed set on a tour of most of Yorkshire, and directed May to the right third-class carriage for Bradford Exchange, where she would change for Halifax.

She had the compartment to herself. The dusty moquette was completely undistinguished, she decided: dark and light blue flowers emerging from goblets that looked like the FA Cup. It was literally florid, suggesting some outdated drawing room.

May read more of *Cakes and Ale*, which was better than *Ashenden*. The novel was partly about sex (hence its great success), but it was also about literature: the main character showed you how to behave as a famous author. Another character showed you how not to, and so May read the book in the hope that it might one day be instructive. There was also Mrs Barton Trafford, that patron of the arts. Mrs Henderson could be one of those, May had been thinking.

When she looked up from the book the houses had given way to the strange landscape around Peterborough, the result of brick-making: ragged, shallow lakes bordered by mounds of earth as if the excavation had taken place only yesterday. There were more fishermen than usual trying their luck, and the water glinted with a certain promise.

After Peterborough, as the train skirted a golden meadow with two black horses in it, May realised what the piece of moquette had reminded her of when she first saw it: the cover of a certain edition of *Black Beauty*: the black horse in the yellow field, and the moquette's other colour, the purply blue, had been present as a border around the image. The colours made you see the sheer blackness of the horse.

A more northern version of summer was now becoming evident: not only horses in fields, but also a cricket match and a party of cheerful men emerging from lineside woodland holding shotguns. At Doncaster it was 10.15, according to the clock on the big office to the left of the station. Pontefract and Wakefield followed, the train's engine bringing its smoke and steam to towns that already had quite enough of those things. By some railway miracle Leeds was avoided.

May changed trains beneath the great glass roof of Bradford Exchange, which was not being as successful as usual at keeping the sun at bay. There was at least one mill in Bradford that made moquette, she believed, but with only ten minutes before her connection there was no point walking into town.

The next train boasted several moquettes, all depicting masses of gloomy flowers. They seemed to clash with almost everybody sitting on them, especially the younger, more modern people. In particular, they looked too genteel for the working men, including one oily fellow wearing a blue boiler suit beneath a black and greasy suit coat. The moquette colours and patterns on this train were so hectic, May reflected, they probably did hide the dirt.

When – the hills and mills rising steeply on both sides – a ticket inspector came along, May asked, 'Who do you think designed this moquette?'

'This what?'

'This moquette – this seat covering.' She indicated their pinkish surroundings.

'Some high-up's wife, I should imagine.'

They were on the outskirts of Halifax, passing the great industrial castles. There was something unfamiliar in the air above them: blueness, and there were not enough people in the streets. At last it dawned on May: the single word Ellie had been trying to communicate to her at Tottenham Court Road. She should have known it from the shape her lips made: 'Wakes'. The second weeks of August was Wakes week in Halifax, when most of the mills and factories closed so the workers could go to the seaside – Blackpool being the standard option, although Scarborough had a following among more adventurous types. Ellie had been trying to warn May that her journey would be wasted. But not every mill closed for Wakes. May had a feeling that of the two she intended visiting – Ramsden's, the chief moquette maker in the country, and the smaller Ambler's Mill – one of them at least stayed open.

As a child, May had usually gone away with her parents during Wakes Week, but not on a Wakes holiday per se. These applied to the factories and mills, whereas May's mother had been a nurse, at St Luke's Hospital, her father a teacher of maths at the Modern School who had then, for reasons best known to himself, become a tram driver for the Corporation.

You didn't walk out of Halifax Old Station so much as climb out of it, since it was at the bottom of one of Halifax's many steep roads, Horton Street. As May climbed she kept turning around to survey the town, the view improving – or at least expanding – all the time. After a couple of minutes she could take in about half the town, which she regarded with a new incredulity. She felt a strong urge to take Halifax in hand: flatten it out, as you would a ruched carpet; lop the tops off some chimneys, boost a few others so there might be at least a rough equivalence among them. Not all the mills were inoperative: a few plumes of smoke rose, as if to prove that the summer's victory had not quite been a clean sweep.

Horton Road rose west from the station; looking to the north and west May could see Dean Clough Mill, like a giant immobile liner, all its chimneys smoking. That was owned by the Crossleys, who made carpets and were considered good employers but had no time for Wakes. Looking south she saw Ramsden's Mill in its groove, a sunken grey street where once a stream had run, and it was working. Or was it? She was confused by a steam train hurrying past it. (May, too, would have crossed in front of Ramsden's had her train not terminated at Halifax Old.) Yes, steam and smoke continued to accumulate over Ramsden's even after the train had gone.

May looked north-east, towards Beacon Hill, which gradually became greener as the grey stone buildings thinned out. Among the last of them was Ambler's Mill; you could just about see the descending stream that had once powered it. At that moment nothing seemed to be powering the mill and, as if to prove the point, a pure-white cloud floated unsullied over its roofs. So Amblers was not weaving and not spinning. Would it be worth going there?

A tram went past, heading downhill – and surely too fast. But after her father's accident all the downhill trams looked too fast for May. The side of the tram acclaimed Ty-Phoo Tea ('For Indigestion'.) The one driven by her father, number 74, had proclaimed READ THE HALIFAX COURIER, at first to the passing pedestrians as intended, then to the skies, number 74 having run out of control and landed on its side. It had happened because the current failed (and because Horton Road was too steep). The Board of Trade Enquiry had exempted her father from all responsibility, so he had received the 'pay-out', to compensate for the resulting incapacity, the difficulty in walking those streets whose steepness had caused the injury in the first place. In view of this you'd think he would have wanted to leave Halifax in favour of a more horizontal town. Instead he had encouraged *May* to leave. A bus now went past, also downhill, but looking more stable – smug, almost.

The trams were beautiful things when they remained upright: cream and blue – 'Prussian Blue', she remembered it was called – were the colours, whereas the buses were green, cream and orange, a brasher livery, and here came another, easily ascending Horton Street; they were taking over the town. In truth neither livery suited Halifax as well as the red buses suited London. Almost any colour seemed arbitrarily imposed on the grey and black of Halifax buildings. Over the road was a shuttered warehouse. 'Holroyd, Artificial Silks', read the plaque on the door. What on earth were artificial silks? She came to the main post office, which looked like a church. They had an electric fan going in there, even though there were no queues at the counters. Continuing up, she passed a bread van, all the doors open, all the bread inside – and nobody about to steal it.

May was heading north. Whenever she went from London to Halifax she exchanged 'King's Cross' for the less possessive '*King* Cross', the district of terraced houses high in the north of the town where she'd grown up and where her father still lived. It was one of the larger houses, with three bedrooms and a garden, where May's father tried to perpetuate the flower beds of his late wife, in order that they might occasionally be cut and taken to her grave.

The short street was deserted except for her father's immediate neighbour, Miss Atkinson, a single woman – jolly, but self-contained. She stood in front of her doorstep breathing in the summer air. She wasn't surprised to see May, who was a regular returnee. 'Hello, dear,' she said. 'I'm just enjoying the peace and quiet. It's so lovely when everyone's gone.'

'I'd forgotten it was Wakes.'

'That's living in London for you. I like your hat, dear.'

'Thanks,' said May, who wondered whether it would come over as patronising to say that she liked Miss Atkinson's pinny. She decided that 'You're looking well, Mrs Atkinson' was the safer bet.

Her father had opened his front door. He was smiling at these ladylike pleasantries. But what exactly his smiles meant you never really knew. May's talent for enigmatic expressions has been inherited from her father, she believed. He was a handsome, sleepy-eyed man, quite formally dressed. He always wore one of two pinstriped suits, and today it was the better of the two, for May's benefit.

'I see you're not using your stick,' Miss Atkinson said to May's father. 'That's good.'

'Oh, I'm much better, thanks,' he said. 'I'm revolving a stroll up Beacon Hill.' May's dad was formal in speech as well as dress, and he would say 'revolving' instead of 'thinking'. His speech was partly antiquated northern, and partly just *him*.

He did seem better, May thought. He showed her into the front room – the best room, used only for her own visits these days, as far as May could tell. It was as full of light as any lace-curtained room in a Halifax terrace could be, mainly thanks to the wallpaper – ivory and pink stripes.

Two mirrors in the room helped the light. There ought to have been some art on the walls; instead, there were certificates that had been awarded to May, framed ever more expensively as the scale of her supposed achievements grew. It had been so embarrassing when visitors came, because they

95

would be forced to ask about them, and if these visitors had children of their own they would have seen many of the certificates before: the one for swimming a length of Lilly Lane Baths, for example. Everybody in Halifax had that. May was quite surprised her birth certificate wasn't up there.

The one in pride of place on the chimney breast boasted of her scholarship to Princess Mary's. Most of the others flowed from that – signifying essay prizes in English Literature. The ideal outcome would have been a certificate attesting to a university degree, but they really were rare, even for Princess Mary girls. That literary star of Halifax, Phyllis Bentley herself, had only taken something called an 'external' degree from London University, causing May to picture her working in the rain at a desk placed outdoors.

Until the tram turned over May had been contemplating teacher training. With a broken hip, and badly broken left leg, her father needed looking after, however much he denied it. Even as he improved, the pay-out still hadn't come through, so money had to be earned, and May had gone to Quarmby's, where Ellie – who had as many certificates for drawing as May had for writing – was already plotting her path to the Exchange.

May's father brought in cups of tea on a tray. He was walking more freely, but still with that lumbering motion that added ten years to him. He had survived the Western Front but been crocked by municipal Halifax. May often wondered whether something so flimsy as a certificate had accompanied her father's Distinguished Conduct Medal (which she only knew about because his friend from the tram depot, George Wilson, had mentioned it to her).

They exchanged presents.

'Hatchard's of Piccadilly,' mused her father, inspecting the ribbon on his parcel. 'This won't have been cheap.' He began unwrapping. 'I'll be keeping this paper,' he said. 'You'll be seeing it again at Christmas. *The Thin Man* . . .' He turned to the first page; he was actually reading it. 'He's like Chandler, isn't he?' he said eventually. 'I like Chandler.'

'Oh, have I bought the wrong author?'

'No, I like this. This is good.' And he was still reading as he spoke. '. . . Hard-boiled,' he said, apparently with satisfaction, as finally he set the book aside. He handed over his present to her – a book, obviously. May unwrapped *Furnishing the Small Home,* by Margaret Merivale.

'I'm hoping in time, love, to be buying you *Furnishing the* Big *Home.*'

'It's lovely, Dad. Just the thing.' Flicking through it, she saw the very book table that she herself owned, although the one in the book was crowned with a bottle of champagne and a telephone. 'Look, Dad,' she said. 'I've got this very one – from Heal's.'

'Did you get it on HP?'

'Heal's don't do HP, Dad. They're a cut above.' Father and daughter exchanged ambiguous smiles, of which there was a further bout when her father said he had cooked a casserole for the meal they would shortly be eating, as opposed to a stew.

'It's a casserole,' he said, 'because it's cooked in a casserole pot.'

This was another promising development, thought May; the most promising would be for him to find another wife.

'Now look at this,' May said, delving into her bag again. 'It's a piece of moquette.'

'Yes,' he said. 'They don't have it on the trams.' On the trams the drivers didn't have seats at all; they stood up. On the lower decks was leather-like stuff. On the upper the seats were usually wooden, especially if the tram had an open top, which a lot of the Halifax ones did, including number 74. It being a rainy evening, there had been only one person up top, and he had been the sole fatality: a Mr Harrison, a large, heavy man who'd been thrown clean across the road even so. He had been smoking his pipe in the rain. May's father, of course, had sent a long letter to his family that was tantamount to an apology, even though he had nothing to apologise for.

'They have it on the buses,' her father said. 'That's partly why people prefer them.' People also liked the buses because they didn't have to board them in the middle of the road.

'It's on most trains,' said May, 'and on the Underground.'

'You're all right going about late at night on that, are you?'

'I'm sticking with the smokers.'

'Because I *was* thinking of equipping you with my service revolver,' said her father, whose ambiguous smile was not returned by May.

She pictured the gun, which she had covertly inspected many times, lying in the topmost of the drawers neatly inset into his wardrobe, among special things like silk handkerchiefs and her father's best cufflinks. It looked astonishingly American to May, like the things cowboys wore in holsters, and its seriousness as an object was attested to by its weight.

Her father was still examining the piece of moquette. 'I think your mother would have liked this.'

'Oh?'

Her mother had made the room May and her father were sitting in a pleasant place to be, with flowers always on the mantlepiece, but the certificates had so mortified May that she had always taken the furniture for granted. She could see now, however, that the three-piece suite was rather distinguished, with its faded green velvet and trim proportions.

'She liked fabrics,' said her father. 'Spent hours reading furniture catalogues. And then there was the bentwood chair.' He was smiling, but May now recalled that the bentwood chair had been the cause of the only row she had ever heard between her parents. She would have been about ten years old. Her mother had ordered it from Bradford – from Brown & Muff's, the so-called Harrods of the North, evidently at great cost.

'It's still in your bedroom, isn't it?' said May.

'Of course it is,' said her father. 'Go and have a look while I make another pot of tea. See if you think it's up to the London mark.'

May climbed the familiar 13 creaking steps and turned right at the top, rather than left, where her own bedroom lay. May's father still slept in the double bed, of course, and made it immaculately the moment he rose in the morning. And there by the window was the expensive chair, even now the most modern-looking thing in the house – and the most beautiful. It might easily have come from Heal's. It was almost decadently low, so you would have to recline on it. It was exotic, too: black, yellow and red stripes, like a deckchair, or something you would expect to find in some Bedouin's tent. The fabric was not moquette, but something more feminine: linen. May formulated a thought that had never quite come to her before: *my mother loved colour*. She remembered her standing in front of a mirror in a new red dress, a bold choice since her hair was auburn (May's father had once corrected May with uncharacteristic severity when she had called it 'ginger'). Her mother had been risking a clash, flirting with it, but she knew what she was doing. 'A new dress is always such a tonic,' she had said, and she had meant the *colour* of a new dress. Before she went back downstairs May glanced over to the wardrobe, which harboured the gun.

'Well?' said her father, pouring fresh tea.

'It's up to the London mark,' said May, 'as you know perfectly well. It occurs to me that I've never seen a nicer armchair, and I've seen a lot.'

Her father picked up the moquette again. She thought he was about to hand it back to her, but he wasn't finished with it yet. 'Do you remember the sunny train?'

May did not, rather alarmingly.

'Well, it was a sunny *carriage*. We were off to Scarborough. The seats had triangular patterns, blue and green. It was quite early in the morning, and the sun was coming in from a high angle. You ran your finger over the seat, because the sunbeams were coming in at the same angle as the pattern. You said, "It's very sunny, this train", just as the ticket inspector came along.'

Now May remembered. '—And he said, "That's down to my disposition," and I didn't know what he meant!'

'Which is fair enough, since you were five.'

Yes, that had been the definitive Scarborough trip: the light always behaving correctly, making the beach golden, sea and sky equally blue, the flowers (the reason her mother loved Scarborough) almost unnaturally vivid; then the return to the station, with the clockface in the clocktower gaslit against the night sky and everybody cheerful all day, as though taking their cue from the ticket inspector. But it had been the pattern in the carriage that had started it all.

Her father handed back the moquette. 'I can't remember why you've got this,' he said.

That was because she hadn't told him, and now she couldn't. She couldn't tell him the truth, anyway. She would in effect be saying that she was looking for a murderer, and that a lot of people in the milieu of the murdered man knew what she was about. Her father would insist she take the gun; he would probably also propose returning to London with her, in the role of bodyguard. No, the whole thing must be presented as fiction.

So May said she was working on one of her North–South tales, featuring a character called Janet Dawson, a May-like person, perpetually undecided about whether to live in London or Halifax. *The Piece of Moquette*, she said the story would be called – and she wanted to do some research by seeing the inside of a textile mill or two, preferably Ramsden's and Ambler's. She said she was thinking of entering the story in a competition, inviting her father to envisage another certificate on the wall. 'Do you think I'm on the right track with Ramsden's and Ambler's?'

'I do,' said her father. 'Ramsden's is working. Ambler's won't be weaving, but there might be a few in. I'll come with you. The walk'll do me good.'

'You can't possibly walk it.'

'I've been told to walk as much as possible,' he said, which May didn't believe. Her father had only proposed walking to lessen May's guilt about living in London.

'Really, don't bother, Dad. I won't be good company for you. I've got things to think through about the story and so on.'

He nodded patiently. Nothing must impede his daughter's singular imagination. They went through to the parlour, where her father had laid the tablecloth and there was butter, not margarine, on the table, which did nothing to lessen May's guilt at her disingenuousness.

11

Ramsden's was working, and working hard, it seemed to May, who glimpsed the weaving floor briefly while being shown along a cool white corridor. Through open double doors she had seen – and been momentarily deafened by – what appeared to be a great tangle of shaking looms attended by white-coated figures, and all operating beneath the cats' cradle of motorised belts that powered them. She hadn't had time for a proper look; she was trailing behind a very efficient receptionist or secretary who had listened to May's strange story as if it were a perfectly routine matter before pronouncing, 'You need the design manager.'

After the weaving floor the design office was remarkably peaceful. Long metal tables were partly covered in what looked like tablecloths too small for them. There were also the great hairy books: moquette sample books. Some were being inspected by two men, one periodically holding a small square of thick glass up to his right eye as he leant close to the material. Trolleys piled with rolls of moquette wrapped in grey hessian were parked between the tables.

'Mr Thornton,' the secretary called to the man accompanying the eyeglass man. 'This young lady would like to ask you a question.' Mr Thornton was like a male equivalent of the secretary: efficient in a black suit.

'Good afternoon, miss. How might I help?' He had spoken politely, but with a glance at his watch.

May showed him her moquette and told him her story. At the right moment she also produced Sergeant Price's card.

'How extraordinary,' said Mr Thornton when she'd finished, although he didn't *look* amazed, and he was examining Price's card as though he suspected a forgery. But the eyeglass man, who was more crumpled and comfortable-looking, was grinning and appeared to be finding the whole thing quite a lark. Mr Thornton said, 'Unfortunately, it's not something we can assist you with, Miss Mitton. Your enquiry is not quite an official one. You might be acting for a professional rival of ours, do you see?'

'Of course, we know you're not *really*,' said the eyeglass man. He was about 50, with longish silver hair, and reminded May of a certain Edwardian prime minister. Mr Asquith, that was it, and partly because he wore a fob watch in his waistcoat.

'It would be quite different' said Mr Thornton, 'if the policeman you mentioned were to call in personally.' It seemed he did not quite *believe* in Detective Sergeant Price.

May must embark on a bluff, even at the risk of losing the card. She proffered it to Mr Thornton a second time – here, take it – and told her second lie of the day. 'If you wouldn't mind calling Detective Inspector Price? He gave me his card to hand to people who wouldn't speak to me direct.'

Mr Thornton, clearly a very correct person, was trying to decide the most correct course of action, evidently with some difficulty. He turned in perplexity to the eyeglass man who, still smiling broadly, stepped forward to become properly part of the conversation. 'So this Price fellow gave you lots of cards to dole out to uncooperative parties, did he?' He sounded pleasantly confident, with the Yorkshire equivalent of an upper-class accent, and May realised that he, and not design manager Thornton, was the senior party here.

'This is the first time I've had to give one out,' she said, which was not quite a lie.

'Well, you needn't bother, miss,' he said, smiling. 'I can assure you that your piece of moquette is not one of ours.'

Having tricked or bullied the two men into this admission, May did not feel able to probe further, and it was something, after all, to have ruled out the major moquette maker in the country.

May saw that the eyeglass the man held was contained in a silver frame, and he was now attaching it to the chain of his watch. His glance at the time was quite open and without Thornton's furtiveness. He turned to Thornton. 'We have ten minutes before conference, don't we?' Thornton nodded reluctantly.

'You're a Halifax lass,' the eyeglass man said to May. 'Presumably you've seen a weaving floor before?'

'I saw yours just now – only a glimpse.'

'Would you like a proper look?'

'That would be very kind,' said May.

'I'm Arthur,' the man said. 'Paul and I have to nip through to the card room for a minute. I'll come back here to collect you and we'll have a – well, an eight-minute tour. No need to wait, Ethel.'

So he *must* be a high-up, to command his colleagues in this way, and use their first names. After the two men had left, May said to Ethel the secretary, 'What's that gentleman's surname, if you don't mind my asking?'

'That's Mr Ramsden.'

'So he owns the mill?'

'Yes, but you won't hear that from him.'

'Will it be quite all right to ask him questions?'

'*Quite* all right, if you can make yourself heard.'

Alone in the design office May reflected that, if she'd been making a story of these events, she'd have Ethel in love with the rich, kindly Arthur, unfortunately for Paul, who saw in Ethel a possible soulmate for himself, both being so formal and efficient.

The pattern books on the table reminded May of children's cloth books, but these much thicker volumes contained no pictures, unless you counted flowers and goblets. The moquettes had labels stitched to them on which were written long numbers divided by slashes and dashes. Each moquette suggested a railway-compartment scene: a pompous man smoking a pipe was clearly meant to be sitting on this military-looking red and gold moquette, whereas an elderly lady would be asleep on this dusky grey and blue one. May wondered who might suit her own moquette. A rather elegant family going on holiday, perhaps? But she could imagine no connection between any such family and a murder.

'All set, dear?' came Mr Ramsden's voice's from behind her.

May moved away quickly from the sample books. She

didn't want Mr Ramsden to think she was still seeking a match for her own moquette. But he seemed amiability itself, to the extent that another thought occurred to May. Now that he'd got rid of his two colleagues, would he feel at liberty to disclose some secret information he'd been keeping back?

The weaving floor was the biggest room May had ever been in. It would take at least five minutes to walk to the far end. There was an unexpected softness in the air – an elusive waxy, or soapy, smell. Great waterfalls of light came in through the high windows, making all those who attended the looms – mainly women – look pale. They didn't seem unhappy, though: they smiled as they communicated by rather graceful gestures, necessitated by the relentless shuddering, clattering and crashing of the looms. Not all the looms made moquette, May had already gathered, but they all went about their allotted tasks with ferocity, as if it were necessary to make enough material to cover the entire world by tomorrow morning. And they worked in a blur, going too fast for the human eye.

Great fans of jerking rods rose from them or descended towards them, controlled somehow from above by clumsily rolling cards punched with holes, like tombolas or the paper rolls that govern a pianola. Some of these rods seemed to be trying to lift up the loom, almost as if agitated at their failure to do so. Seeing May's puzzlement, Mr Ramsden said something about how the rods were lifting and lowering the warp threads. Yes, of course, warp and weft – the elements not only of weaving but also of Halifax.

Mr Ramsden, shouting now, was offering some further explanation as they progressed down the central aisle of the shed. May shook her head to indicate that she couldn't hear. He tried again: 'It's the weft that makes the pattern!' and she heard that, but it seemed to be an abbreviation of what he'd said earlier, and as she thought back over his previous speech she understood. He had said, 'The weft makes the pattern *when it runs over the warp.*' Over, not under. When it ran under, it was invisible. So the pattern, May realised, must be made by the tiny lateral strokes of the visible weft.

You really couldn't see the thing carrying the weft. It was flying back and forth in the belly of the machines and presumably accounting for their seeming to rock from side to side, but there was an extraordinary contrast to all this violence in the way the moquette peacefully emerged from the front of the machines, first like a moving tablecloth on a kind of shelf and then neatly rolling up. How could such quaking masses of metal produce patterns so dainty and in- tricate? And all the patterns coming off the machines seemed remarkable to May, because they appeared to have been produced by magic. Watching all the emerging patterns she suddenly found herself on the brink of tears: the geomet- rical shapes at every angle, the rivers of flowers and leaves in every hue from canary yellow to pale ochre, mysterious patterns suggesting seashells or fossils, sometimes attended by their own shadows or reflections – all conceived with the same purpose: to make people happy. And then May saw an old friend: the up-and-down red and green leaves of Marion Dorn were accumulating on the roll attached to the machine right beside her, as though London was gamely asserting itself amid the Yorkshireness all around. 'I've sat on that, on the Tube!' May shouted.

'It's one of my favourites!' Mr Ramsden shouted back. 'It's called—'

But May couldn't hear what it was called. She cupped her hand to her ear, and this time she heard: '—Leaf . . . or Colindale!'

May could see why 'Leaf', but what was Colindale, she shouted back?

'Tube station.'

'Do all moquettes have names?'

'Most do, and some more than one, but the names are not official!'

It must be the long numbers that are official, May thought.

'The Underground people like red and green!' shouted Mr Ramsden. 'The red symbolises the town, the green the country! They set a big store by green! They think it's—'

But May couldn't catch the last word. She cupped her ear again.

'Serene!'

Some of the looms were embellished with extra wires that seemed to be fussily picking away at the emerging moquette, but May was unable to make out Arthur Ramsden's shouts about these. Something to do with 'cutting'. He sometimes stopped to exchange friendly shouts or gestures with the workers, who generally let the looms get on with it, occasionally making small, delicate interventions, tentatively poking and tweaking before stepping back to admire.

Arthur Ramsden was still talking – or cheerfully shouting – about the London Underground. 'At first their people didn't trust us. They'd come up every couple of weeks to keep tabs on us! Then they saw that we were actually improving their designs! Now, they keep sending us crates of—'

May missed the last word, but it was very likely 'champagne', which seemed confirmed when Mr Ramsden joyously added, 'From Fortnum & Masons!'

May said, 'Of course, you know there are posters in the Tube carriages about how the moquette is made in Halifax!'

'Are there now?' said Mr Ramsden. 'Quite right too! What do you reckon, then?' The sweep of his arm took in the whole of the weaving floor.

May realised she was being invited to make one final summary of the scene. 'It's just so . . . beautiful!' she shouted.

A moment later she and Arthur Ramsden were in another corridor, white and rather bleak but with occasional murky oil paintings of Halifax on the walls. The tour was over; they had left behind the thunder that created its multi-coloured lightning, and they were able to speak normally.

'I hope you've not gone deaf,' said Mr Ramsden. 'Are you off back to London now?'

'After I've been to Ambler's Mill,' said May. 'Will I find anyone there, do you think?'

'Well, I know old man Ambler's on holiday with his two sons and their wives.'

'Not in Blackpool, I suppose?'

Arthur Ramsden shook his head, smiling. 'At their villa in the South of France. But you'll find a few of the maintenance people, and some clerks to keep the place ticking over.'

'Do you think I'll learn anything about this?' said May, tapping her bag with the moquette inside it.

'You've a better chance there than here. We're bigger than Ambler's, but they're older, and they've been in moquette longer. Yours does look rather a museum piece to me. I'll give you one last thought about it. You see, it's rather—'

But now the efficient secretary, Ethel, was bustling towards them. 'Mr Ramsden!' she said, surprisingly sharply. 'They're all waiting in the conference room. You know what old Mr Fowler's like!'

'Sorry, dear,' Mr Ramsden said to May. 'You've never met old Mr Fowler. With luck, you never will. Not a man to be kept waiting!' He shook May's hand and went off along the corridor, while the secretary led May in the opposite direction, towards the exit.

12

In the event, May took a tram to Ambler's, which involved a steep descent followed by a steep ascent. She sat on the wooden top deck, daring the tram to topple over and spill her out. If there was any fresh air to be found in Halifax that afternoon it would be on the top deck of a moving tram, but not more than two or three people joined May during her ride. The heat of the day seemed to be intensifying along with the emptiness of the streets. She kept passing *Halifax Courier* placards that foreswore local news in favour of 'Blackpool and Scarborough Weather Reports' – these for the benefit of the left-behinds, so they could have their holidays vicariously.

Even as she walked up to the main entrance, May wasn't sure whether Ambler's was alive or dead. There was a door-bell, an oddly domestic circumstance, which May rang, and presently it was answered by a jolly man in paint-spattered overalls. He and two others were painting the high walls of the lobby white, which was what it had been before. When May explained what she was about the painter said, 'Well, you want the offices upstairs. Most of that lot are in. You probably want Production. It's written on the door.'

'What about the Design Office?'

The man, who still hadn't put down his paint brush, looked thoughtful. 'I don't think there is one. But Production will know about everything that's *been* designed.'

On the way to the first floor May came to a mezzanine that overlooked the weaving room. It was like staring at a *photograph* of a weaving room, the looms all motionless. Moquette-carrying trolleys were parked in a row directly below her, as in a railway siding. As at Ramsden's, high windows had flooded the room with sunshine. It was as if the light had replaced the people. But then, with a clatter of double doors to the right, a person did appear: a man in a dustcoat walking briskly down the centre aisle. He suddenly clapped his hands in the air as if – May first thought – to express satisfaction at the orderly array of machines around him, but she realised he had killed a flying insect. May didn't think the man had noticed her, but he called up to her, 'Moth!'

May raised a hand in salute before continuing up the stairs. On the next landing she found a corridor of doors, all half open in a casual way. She heard slow typewriting, cheerful voices. She was right next to 'Production Office'. Her light knock was enough to open the door. Inside were three desks and two men – young, but old-fashioned-looking by virtue of their tight suits and moustaches. Two Mr Kippses, May thought. They looked at her with astonishment and delight. One of them stood up and approached. 'Morning, miss, how can we help?'

'Hello, I'm May Mitton. I wanted to ask about a piece of moquette, if you don't mind.'

'We don't mind at all, do we, Steve?' the man said turning

to his colleague. 'Jack Lever.' He held out his hand. 'Please, take a seat.' Jack Lever whirled the chair at the empty desk on it castors to alongside his own. The other, evidently meeker, man, Steve, looked on with interest.

But May didn't want to speak to either of these two. Whoever sat at that unattended desk would be more helpful, because on it lay a magazine called *Startling Detective* – an American production, with the price in a green circle: '15c'. The cover showed a room luridly illuminated in orange and green and a tied-up woman next to an open safe from which, when you looked closely, a snake was emerging. 'The Smooth Operator' was the headline.

May remained standing. 'Who sits here?' she pointed at the empty desk.

'Oh, you don't want to bother about him. That's Fred Bailey. He's still learning the ropes.'

'Actually,' said a voice from behind May, 'I'm senior clerk in Production Outer Office.'

Fred Bailey was a big fellow: less of a Kipps than a Billy Bunter, right down to the bow tie and round wire glasses. When he saw May looking at the magazine, he swept it into the top drawer together with another – possibly even more disreputable – underneath it. 'I'm a bit busy at the moment,' he said, 'but always happy to assist a member of the public.'

May produced her moquette, and Fred Bailey perched on the edge of his desk, listening to her story as though he really were a detective – or at least, a detective in a film. Occasionally he asked clarifying questions. His two colleagues seemed to approve of Fred Bailey's questions, nodding at May's answers as if to say, 'Glad we've got that cleared up, now we can move on.' When the telephone on Jack Lever's desk rang, evidently to summon him away, he left the room with reluctance.

'The first thing I'd say, Miss,' said Fred Bailey when May had finished, 'is that we didn't produce this moquette. The second is – watch yourself.'

May adjudged an enigmatic smile the best response.

'I'd say you'd got hold of an important clue to a murder, and it sounds like you've been associating with the kinds of people who might know the killer or *be* the killer – by which I mean the railway people and art people.'

That, of course, brought Tom back into the frame, so to speak. To steer the conversation in a different direction May said, 'You don't think it was sent to the police by a loony?'

'I doubt it. I daresay – in fact, I know – the police get letters every day from deranged individuals confessing to murders in the news. Famous murders. But this was sent in before the murder came to light, and it's not a notable murder, either. I'll tell you honestly, Miss Mitton. I've never heard of Rex Braddon, alive or dead. So it's not the *normal* type of loony, we can be sure of that.'

'Do you think it's definitely a railway moquette?'

'Most moquette is railway moquette. I'd also say it's been used.'

'You mean, it's been on a train?'

'Yes. It's not cut from a roll just off the loom. I don't say it's been *much* used. It's very clean, but the backing's gone a bit grey and that's the tell-tale sign. Dust, you see. Also, the yellow's faded slightly in the sun.'

The clerk called Steve piped up. 'Can I have a look, Fred?' Bailey walked over to Steve's desk and stood over him as

Steve made his own examination. Clearly, Steve wasn't going to be allowed much time to commune with the precious object. 'It's cut,' he pronounced, eventually.

'Of course it is,' said Bailey, reclaiming the moquette. 'I was just about to mention that. The tufts of a moquette can be uncut, meaning left as loops, or the loops can be cut; or they can be both. This one is entirely cut.'

'Why?'

'Makes it softer.' Steve coloured up slightly at his own boldness.

Now Fred Bailey perched himself on his desk to have his back to Steve. 'A cut moquette,' he continued, 'is more velvety, more comfortable – more luxurious, you could say.'

'So this might be from a first-class carriage?'

'Possibly – perhaps even one of the luxury continental services.'

May pictured seats covered with 'her' moquette rolling away past palm trees. She also thought of the poster by Rex Braddon advertising the night train to Paris.

'Or it might be from a Pullman,' said Bailey. 'Cut moquette has richer colours, like this very vivid yellow, and the Pullman carriages are known for their striking colours.'

What did May know about Pullmans? They were luxury railway carriages, liable to crop up anywhere – even on trains to Halifax. You had to pay extra for them, and when on board you were practically forced to eat a meal. So Pullmans were to be avoided. 'Who makes the Pullman carriages?'

'The Pullman company. It's an American outfit, but with a branch over here.'

'A subsidiary,' said Steve.

'Steve reckons he knows about the railways,' Fred Bailey said, pushing his glasses up his nose. 'But you need to talk to a real specialist on the Pullmans and the luxury trains. Why not try the people at the *Railway Magazine* when you're back in London?'

'Those chaps won't talk to you,' said Steve. May craned around the sizeable form of Fred Bailey for a better look at Steve, whose sly interventions suggested he was something of a dark horse.

'Why not?'

Steve flushed again. 'Too busy. There's another, smaller magazine you should try. The editor's probably the top railway brain in the country. He *used* to work on the *Railway Mag*, but then he struck out on his own.'

'What's his name – and where is he now?'

But Steve was shaking his head. 'Sorry, miss. I just can't remember.'

Throughout this exchange Fred Bailey had been polishing his glasses, as if to prove its unimportance. 'As I say, miss, you need an expert. Not somebody who thinks he knows an expert but turns out doesn't.' He slid off his desk and offered his hand to May. 'I'll show you out.'

'I've remembered the magazine, miss,' said Steve. 'The *Railway Digest*.'

That was where Tom worked. It seemed impossible to keep him out of the picture. Had he mentioned the editor – his boss, presumably? May thought he had, but only incidentally. He had certainly not suggested he might be consulted about the moquette. Why not? Perhaps he didn't rate the man as highly as Steve did? But May thought Steve was probably an objective observer of the railway scene. May's familiar anxiety returned. *Perhaps Tom didn't want her to discover the truth about the moquette.*

May realised that Steve and Fred Bailey were waiting for her to speak. 'I was just going to ask if it might be that one,' she said, causing Steve to give a strange, awed gulp.

Fred Bailey, waiting at the door, was obviously determined that Steve should not have the last word. 'Let me just give you a recap of what I think – from the forensic angle, so to speak?'

'What's *that* when it's at home, Fred?' said Steve, emboldened by his recent success.

Ignoring the question, Fred Bailey said, 'We're looking at a piece of moquette that's been used for a short time in some quite smart carriage. Possibly a Pullman, or first-class. And here's another thing: I reckon it's come from a train down south, not up here.'

'What makes you say that?'

'The colour – especially the yellow. It shows the dirt, or would do if a dirty person ever sat on it. Now, nothing against Northerners. You've obviously one yourself, as am I.'

'And me,' said Steve.

'But the North,' Fred Bailey continued, 'is industrial. You've got miners, fitters, mechanics, all sorts of grubby blokes sitting on your train seats . . . So – bright yellow? To be avoided, miss, but perfectly in order down south, especially if your likely passenger is of the Pullman or first-class sort. And another thing that makes me think it's a southern bit of material is the way it's faded in the sun. Not a problem often encountered on our northern trains, more's the pity.'

May wondered whether these insights into her piece of

moquette were similar to the ones Mr Ramsden would have vouchsafed, had he had the time. Yes, she thought.

'Now, these are only my deductions, miss,' said Fred Bailey, polishing his glasses again, 'but I doubt you'll find them contradicted by your *Railway Digest* chap.'

'Thank you, Fred,' said May. 'I doubt they will be. By the way, have you ever considered joining the police? The detective branch, I mean? I think they'd have you like a shot.'

'You're not the first person to say that, miss.'

As Fred Bailey led May along the corridor towards the lobby Steve called after them, 'You shouldn't compliment him like that, miss. It goes right to his head.'

13

Quarmby's was on Corn Market. When May arrived there, she had only just over an hour till her train, and it would take her 20 minutes to get back to the station. So she climbed the stairs fast to the top-floor offices. She didn't need to look at the succeeding floors: she would only encounter her former colleagues, and the question of whether to talk up or down her London experience. As to the merchandise, she knew what she would see: too much over-elaborate brown furniture of the kind Margaret Merivale would disapprove of; the dusty carpet bazaar with too many floral sprawls, such as she had seen on the train coming up; the cluttered counters in Perfumes, Hosiery and Millinery, under the too-low, ornate cream ceilings, with the hot white globe lights dangling down, and the shelf or niche running around all the walls at the height of about ten feet, on which were propped an assortment of decorations including busts of town dignitaries, obscure trophies, potted palms.

But visitors to the clothing floor would have found themselves in a different world: the weird Art Deco lights of orange marbled glass; wood-panelled walls, large, vigorous plants at regular intervals, and seemingly too few clothes on the elegant wooden mannequins. But these clothes were of the best quality, as the assistants knew very well, so the clothing floor staff were the happiest and most confident in Quarmby's, and this was all the doing of Mrs Henderson.

On the top floor was a customer reception, known to the staff as the complaints counter. A young woman May did not recognise sat behind it. She rose to her feet, as she was obliged to, but with a certain hauteur. Her red dress was angular, the kind of thing worn by a secretary in an American film. 'Instead of "How might I assist you, ma'am?", she said, 'You're an Exchange girl, aren't you? I joined just before you left.'

The girl was called Sally. She admitted she'd never been to London but talked about it all the way along the red carpet that led to the door of Mrs Henderson's office. Sally knocked lightly. 'I might give the Exchange a whirl myself.' As Mrs Henderson called 'Enter' she spun away with a fashion model's self-conscious walk.

May had gambled on Mrs Henderson not being in Blackpool. It was quite impossible to imagine her there. Monte Carlo or Cannes, yes. Mrs Henderson's office had similar Deco stylings to the clothes floors, and the same orange glow, cosy and dreamlike. She had been standing at the window, through which May could see a single column of smoke bending in the pale-blue air as though genuflecting towards Mrs Henderson. 'Hello, darling!' she said. 'What a lovely surprise. You're looking wonderfully well. I love your bag, and your hat.'

May thought the first compliment genuine, the second possibly not. There was little point reciprocating with compliments about Mrs Henderson's appearance. You'd be there all day. She resembled a cat, as May did, which was why May had never been quite as nervous of her as she perhaps ought to have been, but Mrs Henderson was the more finished feline article, in that her eyes were green, under lids delicately coloured blue-grey. She kept her eyebrows thick, of course, like Léa in *Chéri*. She wore a brown crepe afternoon dress with a pleated skirt and lace collar. The brown was quite sombre but worked wonders with her eyes, and her face was as pretty as the lace collar.

'That really is a gorgeous hat,' said Mrs Henderson. 'Suits you perfectly. Pert.'

'Thanks,' said May. 'I'd sort of got out of the habit of wearing hats in London. People often don't, in the West End anyhow.'

'So it's a diplomatic hat for Halifax? How are you liking London?'

'Oh, greatly.'

'Would you care for a coffee, dear?' It was typical of Mrs Henderson to offer coffee and not tea. May shook her head. 'Would you like to sit down, at least?'

There was a cream Art Deco armchair in the corner, shaped somewhat like a scallop shell. Sitting on it would be like sitting on a work of art. She shook her head again. 'It's only a flying visit. I must get the train back.'

'What department have they got you in?'

'Furnishings.'

'Furnishings? You should be in Fashion! Men's especially. You set records every day when you were here. It was the way you played so hard to get. On behalf of the clothes, I mean, but also on behalf of yourself. Are you courting?'

'No, but . . . Well, no.'

'There's a boy, I can tell.'

May did not want to think about Tom just then but, not wanting to appear dull in Mrs Henderson's eyes, she said, 'Perhaps. He's American. From New York.'

'Profession?'

'Journalist.'

'What about his family?'

'His father's a motor manufacturer.'

'Careful, dear, you're making me jealous.'

'I think he's slightly estranged from his father.'

'All the best young men are.'

No, it was impossible to pretend that Tom was anything as straightforward as a romantic prospect.

'But how are *you*, Mrs Henderson?

'A little blue, when I read the news. People are trying to sell me dresses that look like army uniforms: depressing square shoulders. Do you miss Halifax at all, dear?'

'Being in London brings its merits into focus.'

'Very diplomatic, like your hat.'

'What have you been reading, Mrs Henderson?'

'*The Great Gatsby*, for about the fifth time. *Vile Bodies* by Evelyn Waugh. This is very touching, dear, because you're expecting me to mention something *you* haven't read. And you're still writing?' May told her a little about her 'work'.

'Well, you're going to set the Thames on fire, I just know it. Now. How's Ellie?'

'Well, she got sacked.'

'Oh.' Mrs Henderson was not completely surprised. 'Did she tell someone to get lost or something?'

When May told her what had happened Mrs Henderson sighed. 'When she was here her technique lacked all sophistication. She'd say to a customer, "It looks nice". Then, if they still hesitated, "It looks *really* nice", and if that didn't do the trick she'd say, "I think you should buy it . . . now!" But then she'd suggest matching two colours that made you think she was a genius.'

'She's working at Selfridges now – in Haberdashery. She likes it.'

'Well, Selfridges is so big. Maybe the bosses won't notice her so much. She's drawing, I hope?'

'She goes to a night class,' said May and, setting her bag down on Mrs Henderson's desk, she took out Ellie's sketch. 'Here's one of her latest. She didn't *ask* me to bring it, but I said I wanted to. She said you can keep it if you like.'

Looking at the subject's piggy eyes, Mrs Henderson's beautiful ones seemed to become almost tearful. 'I *will* keep it. Please thank her. It's like Rembrandt, or somebody. Does *she* have a boy?'

'Still the same one – just about.'

'That clerk?'

'He's going to be a lawyer.'

Mrs Henderson pulled a face.

'She's going to try for the RCA. The Royal College of Art.'

'I know what the RCA is, dear.'

'There's an exam, of sorts, but then, of course . . . she'll need money.'

Mrs Henderson was smiling; then she was laughing. May was laughing, too, at her own brazenness.

'You know,' said Mrs Henderson, 'I was starting to think

that London might have made you an even more subtle girl than you were before. I'm glad to be reminded that you're still twenty years old. Let me kiss you.'

The wall clock – yellow in a blue octagon – told May she really ought to be leaving for the station, but she had five minutes to spare, so she produced the moquette. 'Do you like murder stories, Mrs Henderson?'

'I think I'm going to like this one.'

Mrs Henderson took the moquette and brushed its pile, and it was the material itself, rather than the story May told, that seemed to interest her. 'I like this,' she said.

'Why?'

'The root of the word "decoration" is decorous, meaning "correct". Now of course, *I'm* not correct, but the things I buy for this store are correct – and *this* is correct. What I suppose I'm saying,' she said, handing it back, 'is that I can't believe that the person who designed this is a murderer.' She was opening one of the drawers in her desk, and passed May two lipsticks. 'One for you and one for Ellie,' she said. 'It's Chinese Red; be careful with it. A little goes a long way. It might bring your boy out of his shell and scare off that flipping clerk of Ellie's. Now, if she passes the RCA exam, tell her to write to me care of this address.' She handed May a card. The address was in Paris: rue la Fontaine.

'You're moving to Paris?'

'That's it. One has to move to Paris eventually. I just hope Hitler doesn't get there before me.'

'But you'll be coming back to Halifax?'

Mrs Henderson shrugged. 'I'm selling my place, so perhaps not.'

'Then . . . you'll be leaving Quarmby's?' May felt very stupid asking all these questions, but she was in a state of shock.

'Yes, I'll take one last look at the Piece Hall. That's the right way to say goodbye to Halifax, don't you think?'

'But you'll come back, won't you?'

'Maybe, maybe not. Perhaps another Quarmby & Bates will arise on the Boulevard Haussman, or whatever it's called. Those two really do have more money than sense, you know – which is why I've done so well over the years.'

'Do you have friends in Paris, Mrs Henderson?'

'I have *a* friend,' she said, which was exactly what May had hoped she would say. 'Keep in touch, dear.'

They kissed again, and May quitted the building with the coolness and grace that any meeting with Mrs Henderson inculcated, but when she was back on Corn Market she began running for her train. But then she stopped and checked her watch. She had ten minutes in hand after all. She turned on her heel along a side street. She would take a leaf out of Mrs Henderson's book.

The Piece Hall. That was a term she *did* understand. It could hardly be simpler. It denoted a 'piece' of woollen cloth that its weavers had once exhibited for sale in the high galleries around the great courtyard.

The Piece Hall had always reminded May of a Roman amphitheatre. Now it was a marketplace owned by the council. There probably had been a market earlier in the day, a small one in the corner of the courtyard. All that remained were two men sweeping up rubbish, and a third climbing into the cab of a lorry. He started the engine, and its roar echoed around the high, empty galleries. With the parched grass of the hills behind Halifax seemed grandly, scruffily Italian. May pictured those galleries hung with coloured cloths, all proclaiming the individual visions of their weavers, all those colours and patterns designed to lift the spirits like so many carefully tended flowers. That Yorkshire phrase: *a bit of all right*. Yes, Halifax was a bit of all right, and May made a mental apology for having ever thought anything else.

Now it *was* time to run to the station.

The train for Bradford Exchange was delayed, however. Amid the half-dozen sleepy platforms of Halifax Old Station a silent and sad-looking family were the only other people waiting for the train. A marbling of pink in the sky over Halifax, the last beautiful effect of the day, was wasted on the empty town.

On the platform opposite a long, soot-blackened building incorporated a recess into which a row of wooden telephone boxes had been fitted. May picked up her bag and crossed the footbridge. Halfway over she halted to look along the empty line, and then went on, confirmed her in her desire to act. She must find out more about Tom, and she could do so at the same time as consulting his boss about the moquette. Her suspicions about Tom's connection to Rex Braddon meant she didn't want to be alone with him, but there could be no danger in seeing him in a clattering, crowded magazine office.

She took his card from her purse, and enough change for a trunk call. It was the old-fashioned sort of phone, but when she picked up the earpiece and joggled the hook the operator was there straight away, and only a few seconds after May had read out the number she heard, '*Railway Digest*, Crosby speaking.' The familiar slight hoarseness, the American swing of his speech.

'Hello, Tom,' May said. It was the first time she'd called him by his name. Of course, he called her 'May' all the time, but possibly only as a sort of nervous reflex.

'May. What a lovely surprise.' He *sounded* like he meant it.

'You asked me to call you.'

'I . . . Yes. But I didn't think . . .'

He didn't think I would. She pictured him tousling his hair.

'I wanted to see you,' he said. 'Something a bit funny happened.' Clearly he meant 'funny' in the sense of not funny at all. 'But I know you're on vacation this week.'

'That's right. I'm calling from Halifax.'

A pause. Was he recollecting that she'd said she would be going to Halifax?

'May,' he said, 'I think you're taking a chance by pursuing this moquette business.'

She thought of the night before – the shadowy comings and goings. 'And what makes you say that?'

'Here's the thing, May . . .' And he began to explain. At least, that's what May assumed he was doing, but he was suddenly far away amid the chaotic din of what sounded a radio dial turning.

'Tom,' she said, 'I can't hear you.'

'May,' he said, 'can you hear me?' Then she thought she heard him say, 'Come by the office tomorrow.'

'What time?'

Perhaps he had heard this, because he said, 'I'll be here all day.'

The operator was now speaking, but all May got was the regretful tone of her voice before the line went dead.

The train came in, and May almost wished it hadn't, because it might be taking her back to danger. After Bradford there was a buffet car – quite swanky with polished chrome and leather seats – and May had it all to herself. She ordered a small sherry and a cheese sandwich. The attendant, a bow-tied, methodical-looking man who'd been making notes on a small pad, gave her the sherry and came back with the sandwich.

'There's a Pullman train that goes to Halifax, isn't there?' May asked him.

'That's right, a through carriage of the *Yorkshire Pullman*.'

But May had only brought that up as a staging post to another question.

'What are the main southern Pullmans?'

'You mean on the Southern Railway?'

'Maybe.'

'There are lots of trains with Pullman carriages. And the *Brighton Belle* is *all* Pullman, of course.'

May had heard of that.

'And there are Pullmans on the London Underground.'

'On the Tube, you mean?'

'Not exactly. It's not all "Tubes" on the Underground, you know. Ever heard of the Metropolitan Line? That's just like a big railway, or likes to think it is. It runs two Pullman carriages up to spots like Chesham and Aylesbury. You can pick them up from Baker Street half a dozen times a day.'

Then May would do that, because here was a Pullman more or less on her doorstep. Perhaps she could fit in in before her visit to the *Railway Digest*.

May remained in the buffet car; she found the presence of the methodical man reassuring. At Peterborough she heard a train announced for Oxford. She thought of Guy Cavanagh's heckle during the speech of Aubrey West, the Bond Street gallerist. Cavanagh worked in Oxford, so that ought to be another port of call. The thought compounded her anxiety about Tom, and the buffet car attendant seemed to detect this. He walked over holding a bottle of sherry. 'Top you up, miss? We might as well use up that last inch or so left in here.'

There was more than enough for a small sherry.

14

The *London Underground Railway Map* (consulted in May's morning bath) told her that the Northern Line south to King's Cross, then a change to a westbound Metropolitan Line train, would be the best way of getting to Baker Street. But she decided against the Northern Line part because she had a call to make on her way to King's Cross, and because the Northern Line had been the setting of a nightmare she'd had last night.

It was still vivid in her mind even as she descended sunny Haverstock Hill. She'd been explaining to a man sitting beside her, whose face she couldn't see, but which ought to have been reflected in the windows opposite, that she had been 'lumbered' (the very word she had used) with a piece of material that had been 'on a train that had led to a murder' (again, exactly how she'd expressed it).

'Yes,' the man had said. 'I only did it to cause trouble for you.'

'Did the murder, you mean?'

'No. Died.'

And there, finally reflected in the window, was the imperious face of Rex Braddon.

May turned off Haverstock Hill, into Antrim Grove. Here was the small, interestingly modern-shaped Belsize Park Library. It looked like a tramcar, or a giant lozenge. The main librarian, Mr Alexander – as efficient as his tortoiseshell glasses suggested – would order in books he didn't happen to have faster than any Boots' Library, and unlike Boots' Library books Mr Alexander's came free. May asked him about *Impasse*. 'Yes,' he said, 'by Emma Dean. Published seven or eight years ago. Not a popular title. Certainly we've never had it, but I think I can get it from Camden.' When Mr Alexander said that it meant he *would* get it from Camden. 'I'll drop it through your letterbox.' That was the other way Mr Alexander was better than a Boots librarian, although May didn't know whether the service was available to all his customers.

When she stepped out of the library, the increasing goldenness of the day was banishing the memory of her nightmare. On the upper deck of the 63 bus the process was completed. All the windows that could be open were. The moquette had an interesting, elusive pattern: within thin diagonals of light and dark green, circular black shapes were suggested, like berries in a sunlit forest. Its sophistication was touchingly at variance with the cockney chatter coming up from the lower deck.

Beyond Camden London seemed to intensify, like the swelling of a symphony that would reach its climax somewhere near the river, but May got off at King's Cross. The Metropolitan Line platforms were open-air, and the windows of the strange train approaching May sparkled in the sun. It was a new, red train but bigger than those on the deeper lines. Wider at its base than its top, it looked strange and somehow foreign – certainly too exotic to be going to Hammersmith, its stated destination.

Its moquette was green and red, for town and country, just as Mr Ramsden had said. The red was in the form of large diamond shapes superimposed on green and black squares. The red was embellished with black lines, which made it seem roughly painted on, as though by a frayed brush, but May knew this was all part of the design's cleverness. This, it came to her, must be the moquette by Enid Marx that Lucy Palmer had mentioned to her.

May rode the half-empty train through wide, gloomy tunnels to Baker Street. The station bustled as a junction should – like an underground high street. Amid the flower stalls, cafés and shops she found a booking office where she asked for tickets on 'the special Pullman train'.

'And where do you want to *go* on that train?' asked the smiling ticket clerk.

'Chesham.'

The clerk gave her two tickets: an ordinary third-class return, and another with the word 'Pullman' bigger than the word 'Chesham'.

May said, 'Don't you need a first-class ticket to go on a Pullman?'

'*You'll* be quite all right without one,' said the clerk, and May knew better than to ask what he meant by that.

The platform for Chesham was in the open air but over-shadowed by a great white block of flats. Advertisements along the platform appeared to refer to it: 'Make Your Home at Chiltern Court, Baker Street NW1 . . . Direct Access to

Baker Street Underground Station . . . Within Easy Reach of West End Theatres and 14 Golf Courses.'

A locomotive was approaching, not from Chesham but from the bowels of Baker Street – from beneath Chiltern Court, in fact. As it came in past May it gave off heat but no steam or smoke, and it whined shrilly. It was electric, but the creaking wooden carriages it pulled would have been more at home behind a steam engine. Inside there were compartments, their seats upholstered with patterns of small, pretty flowers, mainly red and white, like nursery curtains. A uniformed man was plodding towards her along the corridor. 'Excuse me,' she said. 'This *is* a Pullman train, isn't it?' She didn't trouble to keep the incredulity out of her voice.

'Two Pullman *cars*,' he said, 'that way.'

As the train pulled away she went in search, and came upon a small utopia: a carriage resembling a sumptuous hotel bar, or a sliver of Chiltern Court sent out into the world. A thick-pile geometric carpet of gold and red, silver luggage racks, glass-topped tables with cloths deliberately too small (to show off the glass), pink-shaded electric table lamps, green silk blinds rolled up at the windows – and all this luxury was quite enraging because the chairs, which were freestanding armchairs, had no moquette at all but covers of red leather. Fewer than half the seats were occupied, by people who looked pampered but bored, as though overfamiliar with one another's company. They were all looking at May to see what she would do next.

She remembered that there were two Pullman carriages, so she walked the length of this one to the next. It was slightly different: the carpet was plain green and there was a bar at

the end, at which an elderly waiter was unenthusiastically re-
ceiving a tray from the barman. But the seats were the same.
There were even fewer people in this carriage than the last:
at one table two women talked in low voices while looking
at May; at another a man was returning to his magazine after
a good ten seconds of staring at her.

The waiter came up: 'May I see your ticket, madam?'

There was a menu on the table he showed her to; he sighed
as she read it. The menu offered 'à la carte meal service',
'light à la carte' and a wine list – all at 11.30 in the morning;
and yet the man reading the magazine was indeed drinking
red wine. May said, 'Just a cup of tea, thanks.'

'Pot of tea for one,' and the waiter departed.

May had hoped to avoid the 'pot', since it would cost,
according to the menu, one shilling and five. Beyond the
window neat white houses with red roofs were skimming
past. No factories or mills: these houses were people factories, where families were made. Perhaps May should install
her heroine, Janet Dawson, in one of them, with a boring
husband. She would rebel against the artificiality of the ex-
istence and flee back to Halifax. It occurred to May that this
was, or had been before the war, Metroland. There'd been
a song about it: a man singing about his 'little house' and his
'little wife' – so it must have been satirical.

They had rattled through a couple of stations without
stopping when it occurred to May that she might be trapped
in this costly carriage for a couple of hours. When the waiter
brought the tea, she said, 'When's the first stop?'

'Harrow, madam.'

'What time?'

135

'Eleven fifty-five.'

Well, it was only 20 minutes away. She might as well get something out of the journey, so she took the moquette out of her bag. 'Do you know if this was used as a seat covering in any Pullman carriage?'

'I can't say, madam,' he said in his tired voice.

Behind him May saw the red wine man turning the pages of his magazine. Now she could read the title: *Railway Digest*. The man smiled wolfishly at her, as if to confirm that the solution to the mystery – not only of the moquette but also of Tom Crosby – would indeed be disclosed to her later at its offices. *It had better be*, May thought, *otherwise I'm giving up the whole damn quest*.

She alighted at Harrow, whose concrete and brick station had a long waiting room shaped like a Murray Mint where she thought she might shelter from the sun. But it was suffocatingly hot, and she stayed no longer than the time it took to read a poster headlined, 'Looking for a house? Try Rickmansworth', which seemed disloyal to Harrow.

The train that eventually came in was a stubby, American-looking thing, electric and painted a lurid, self-conscious maroon. The zig-zag moquette in the compartment she boarded was, she supposed, 'jazzy' – that over-familiar notion. A 'jazzy' fabric would suggest daring in a Metroland home, whose occupants surely did not experience the real 'jazz', in noisy nightclubs late at night. The railway timetables would not permit it. They might at best listen to jazz music on their radios, and May could see the aerials bristling from the red roofs as the train neared Baker Street, the Metroland prisoners desperately reaching out to the wider world.

May was becoming quite disgusted with herself. It was not fitting that a shopgirl should be so snobbish. But it wasn't as if she opposed all the artificiality or snobbery of the modern world. Today people – Londoners especially – lived in a designed world, and the right design could make a person happy. Her own moquette – which evidently did not belong in either the old or new world of the Metropolitan Railway – was, she believed, in that uplifting category, but just now it wasn't making her happy so much as impatient. She needed to know where it came from, and the speed with which her train was hurtling back to Baker Street did suggest that some revelation lay in wait.

Back at King's Cross May vaguely thought the Bank Branch of the Northern Line would take her in the direction of Fleet Street, but walking to the Tube station she saw a trolleybus destined for 'Holborn Circus (via Farringdon Road)'. Number 517 – were there really another 516 trolleybuses in London, May wondered as she ran for it holding her hat? You didn't see many of these weird, electrified buses, and she had not been on one before.

The trolleybus seemed to float her silently into the middle of town. The moquette was charmingly self-deprecating, suggestive of faded autumn leaves blown into a pond, but it was not 'hers'. At Holborn Circus the conductor – a bit more refined, she thought, than the average bus conductor – directed May to Fleet Street. She knew she'd arrived when everyone was scurrying self-importantly past her. *Deadlines*, she thought. *The Daily Express*, the paper Tom so admired, occupied a veritable skyscraper with a façade like a black mirror.

The dome of St Paul's frowned down at Fleet Street – the great cathedral, surely, did not approve. Fleet Street was a bit too pleased with itself.

Whitefriars Street was off to the left, and the building housing the *Railway Digest* was a perfunctory sort of place. No reception, just a noticeboard giving a list of publications and the floors they were on. Some sounded interesting (*Life and Letters*, *Poetry Index*); most didn't. It seemed they were all under the auspices of a company whose name had recently been changed, the name of the old one having been over-painted with 'Redwood & Gilmour Publishing Co.' The *Railway Digest* was on the top floor.

The stairs were oddly primitive: dark, steep and winding like the stairs in a church tower. Tom Crosby answered her knock as quickly as he'd answered her telephone call. He looked the same as he had before, only more so: more elegantly dishevelled in his pale clothes and more handsome. He held out his hand, but the formality was undermined by his 'Hi, May! Sorry about the state of this place.'

It was one room, apart from a wood and glass enclosure next to the door. Nobody sat at the desk in there, which had a coal scuttle on it, and the wider office also seemed deserted. It appeared, therefore, that May was alone with the man who might have killed Rex Braddon. The room was dark green. Two long tables were strewn with papers. Thin tartan curtains were half-closed, yellow sunlight filtering through to accidentally decorative effect. A stone sink beneath the windows had only one tap and ill-assorted glasses and cups on a crude shelf above it.

Tom was beckoning May to his desk in the middle of the

room. She wasn't sure she wanted to follow him, and she might not have had she not then heard the sound of slow typing. It came from the furthest corner, where sat a thin, bespectacled man who hadn't removed his beret even though the room was quite stifling. 'That's Alec,' said Tom. 'Alec, this is May.'

Alec stood and performed a stiff, half-comic bow.

May called back 'Nice to meet you, Alec,' and she meant it. Tom Crosby couldn't murder her now.

'Alec's the sub-editor,' he was saying, 'and a very smart fellow – corrects all my mistakes with a smile. Well, there's the *occasional* grimace, you know? I'd never show my copy to Roy without running it past Alec.'

'It's rather a skeleton staff, isn't it?'

'Uh-huh. Most of the copy comes in from freelancers. Our pages go off today, so another fellow comes in about four to help with that.'

'Where's the editor?'

'The pub,' said Tom. He and Alec exchanged glances. 'Would you like a cup of tea?' He apparently tried to sound as English as possible as he said those last three words, which was quite endearing.

May shook her head. There was a spirit stove on his desk, along with a telephone and some long, narrow documents that, May realised, would eventually become the pages of the magazine. A streamlined stainless steel ash tray was next to a packet of 'Star' cigarettes – a jolting sight, given what the Piccadilly tobacconist had said: a 'nervy sort of chap'. There was also a novel: *Rebecca*, by Daphne du Maurier. This was just out, and by all accounts was likely to be found 'sensational' by railway travellers, or anyone. Nothing on the desk proclaimed 'railways', and very little in the room seemed to. But on the mantelpiece above the fireplace was a green toy locomotive, somewhat collapsed.

Tom had brought up a second chair to sit down on. 'First off, May,' he said, 'are you OK?'

'I'm fine. Explain about this "funny" business, Tom.'

'You know who Kenneth Cooper is, right?'

It was a name May had hoped not to hear again. 'He's a painter,' she said. 'An alcoholic one, if the night before last is anything to go by. I saw him at a private view in Bond Street. I think that's the term. A party, anyhow – to open an exhibition of works by Rex Braddon. I thought I might see you there. Did you not hear of it?'

'Uh-huh,' said Tom. 'I went along.'

'That must have been after I left?'

He nodded again. 'I was behind schedule, May. I'd had a little trouble here.'

'What sort of trouble?'

'Roy. The usual – no need to get into it just now. But Cooper . . . I don't want to alarm you, May, but he was talking about you. I got the lowdown from a woman called Lucy – some kind of artist. She said you'd just left. Apparently when you showed her the moquette you were talking about the police and Cooper was hanging about nearby, and he didn't like what he heard. "Police", I mean. It seems Braddon was his commanding officer in the war, or part of the war. At first Braddon encouraged Cooper to paint, but then they had a falling out.'

'Over what?'

'Braddon had an affair with his wife. Anyhow, next thing

I knew, Cooper was gone, but I couldn't believe he'd just go home – he seemed so fired up. I walked out into Bond Street but he was nowhere to be seen. Then I thought about the guest book or whatever it's called, where everyone wrote their name and address for the gallery's PR.'

'Its what?'

'Public relations. Mail shots. He'd been hanging around near the guest book. I double-checked and there was your address.'

'So you took a taxi?'

'How did you know?'

'I heard the engine outside my window. Did you see him?'

'Uh-huh. He wasn't right outside your place. He was a little way down the road. Figuring out his next move, maybe. But I don't think he was in any state to do anything. He was kind of slumped against a hedge. I went and asked him if he was Cooper. Said we'd just been at the same party. I made out I lived on that same street. I said I thought it was time he went home and got some sleep.'

'What did he say?'

'He made a lunge at me. I told him to beat it. Then I backed off and watched him. After a while he headed back towards the main road.'

'Rosslyn Hill?'

'Yup.'

'And what did you do then?'

'Walked the same way and took a cab home.'

'Why didn't you knock on my door?' said May, who couldn't decide whether she felt slighted or honoured that he had not.

Tom brushed his hair out of his eyes and picked up his cigarettes. He offered the packet to May; she shook her head. When his cigarette was lit Tom leant back, careful to blow his smoke away from her. 'I thought it would be out of line, May. To knock on your door at midnight when we'd only just met. And then if I gave you my reason for turning up, that might have alarmed you. Or you might not have believed me.' He smiled and shrugged. 'And it's not like your light was on.'

She believed he was about to say something else, but there came the sound of the office door opening, and Tom was regarding it with perplexity. 'Roy,' he said.

Roy Williams, editor of the magazine, approached with a pipe in his mouth and a parcel under his arm. He was a strangely shaped man, as if he were smuggling another parcel under his heavy tweed suit coat, a garment surely too hot for the day – which might explain the redness of his big, sagging features. It was an unhealthy red, shot through with grey, like a rotten strawberry.

When Tom introduced May, Williams shook her hand and said, 'Well, well – a young lady in the office. Do you have an interest in railways, dear? We'll soon cure you of that!'

He seemed very amiable and, the redness aside, not overtly drunk. He spoke fast in an upper-class accent, sometimes with the pipe still in his mouth. 'Got a little something for you, Tom,' he said, producing a large book from the parcel. It had a marbled cover of swirling browns and greens. There were no words on the cover, so presumably anyone who picked up this book already knew what was in it. 'Thought this might do for your new book slot. *The Universal Directory of Railways* for nineteen thirty-eight to nine, edited by Major

Bernard Foster, published by the Directory Publishing Company. Has the particulars, Tom, of every important railway in the world including numbers of carriages, wagons and locomotives, number of staff employed, mileages covered, including in tunnels and electrified lines. Eighty pages for the index alone! Now if that's not "sensational", I don't know what is.'

Tom's glance flickered towards May. There was not as much amusement in it as May would have liked. Sensing his colleague's hesitation, Williams said, 'It's a brand-new book, my boy. Out next month. Last month's choice wasn't exactly new, was it? Not saying it wasn't "sensational", mind. It might very well have been!' He turned to May. 'My knowledge of fiction is nil!'

Tom didn't so much stub as stab his cigarette out. 'Here's the thing, Roy . . . We already have our round-up of the railway titles on the back page. I thought we'd agreed that the new page would have a novel every month. I'd lined this one up for the next issue.' He held up *Rebecca*.

'I see. And who is this Rebecca?'

'She's a young woman who marries a rich widower and goes to live in his house in Cornwall.'

Williams bowed his head reverently. 'Great Western territory.'

'The house is . . . kind of haunted by his previous wife.'

'What do you mean by "kind of", Tom?'

'Well, it's not a ghost story, strictly speaking.'

Williams was nodding hard. 'I'm sure some of our readers will find it interesting in any case.' He turned again to May. 'Mustn't be too technical, must we? Simply because this is a *railway* magazine? Bit of light relief every now and again can't possibly do any harm. So, yes, we'll have this *Rosetta* . . .'

'*Rebecca*,' Tom said, with a sharpness May had not heard from him before.

'—We'll have her this month, but perhaps revert to a railway title in the next edition? Does that suit, Tom? Take a look through anyhow, see what you think.' He dropped the great tome onto Tom's desk, and there was a hint of unsteadiness as he walked away.

'How do you like Roy Williams?' Tom whispered to May.

May didn't speak because Tom was obviously straining to hear the conference between Williams and Alec. She got the idea that Alec was politely trying to resist some further suggestion of Williams's.

Williams rested on the mantlepiece and took his pipe out to cough from deep in his chest. 'Tom, my boy', he called across the room, still spluttering, 'you haven't forgotten about the LNER loco stock changes?'

May opened the Gladstone bag to remind Tom of the moquette.

He nodded. 'Let's run it past him. Roy,' he said. 'Got something here to show you.' He pulled up a seat for Williams, and May told an abbreviated version of her story as Williams wheezed, occasionally closing his eyes. She thought at one point he had fallen asleep.

'Curious tale,' he said, opening his eyes when May had finished. 'Of course, I read about the murder of Braddon in the London papers. As I said to Tom, the uncharitable thought did occur that he'd got what he deserved for giving us the run-around.'

May was alarmed. 'How do you mean?'

'Didn't Tom tell you? At the start of July he interviewed Braddon for a feature on . . . railway posters, was it?'

'Among other things', said Tom. 'It was to be a feature on the rise of railway PR' – that strange expression again – 'of which Braddon was a great beneficiary. It wasn't just down to his posters, but a whole bunch of things: illustrations for railway publications, dust jackets for railway books, fliers for excursions —'

Roy was nodding impatiently again. 'It all became academic when he sent us a telegram a week later saying we were not to run the piece, Miss Mitton. Legal action was threatened. We had to remake the magazine on press day, at considerable cost. Our proprietor Mr Redwood was not best pleased.'

When in the Maida Vale pub Tom had first told May about this row with Braddon she had got the idea it was a relatively minor matter. Evidently it was not.

'Let's take a look at this moquette,' said Williams, picking it up. He paused as great coughs shivered his whole body. Eventually he gasped and pronounced, 'I don't think I've ever seen it in *situ*, so to speak, but it reminds me of the sort of fancy stuff you might see on a Pullman.'

'Someone else said that,' said May, thinking of that confident young man, Fred Bailey, and her wasted morning on the Metropolitan. 'How would I find out about Pullman moquettes?'

'Try the firms that make the carriages: Metropolitan-Cammell Carriage in Birmingham, or the Birmingham Railway Carriage and Wagon Company at Smethwick, four miles *west* of Birmingham. Or there's the Pullman works at Brighton, half a mile north of the carriage works of the LBSCR, as was.'

'The London Brighton & South Coast Railway,' Tom said to May. 'The company no longer exists.'

'—Absorbed into the Southern Railway at the 1923 Grouping, my dear.' Williams put his pipe back in his mouth and spoke in a bitten-off way around it. 'Some of its stock is still in use of course, but less and less since electrification.'

They seemed to have entered a tangled railway thicket.

'Come to think of it,' said Williams – he was parting the pile on the moquette with a stained finger – 'this is the kind of fancy upholstery that company went in for.'

'What company?' said May. There'd been so many mentioned.

'The Brighton company,' said Williams. He turned to Tom. 'Of course, we know where to go to see the good old Brighton four- and six-wheelers, don't we? That veritable living museum of the railways?'

Tom nodded, and he and Williams pronounced simultaneously: 'The Isle of Wight.'

If May was going to continue her investigation she would rather do so on the Isle of Wight than in the other place that had come up a lot recently, Birmingham.

'Fifty-five miles of railway on an island only twenty-three miles by twelve, Miss Mitton,' said Williams, pipe waggling in his mouth. 'So there's lots to see. Perhaps Tom here will be your guide? He's due a little time off. Been a little overstrained recently, has young Tom. Alec and I will hold the fort.' With a wave of his pipe, Williams wandered off towards his inner office.

Tom was smiling – a 'nervy' smile, May thought. 'What do you reckon, May? How are you fixed for tomorrow?'

'For the Isle of Wight?' she said, to buy time.

'Uh-huh', he said, scooping his hair back. 'Just a day trip, of course. While the sunny spell continues. I mean, if you're really going to pursue your investigation, it might be as well that you have a bit of back-up.'

May found herself shaking her head. Her suspicions had just been compounded. Tom had had a better reason for killing Rex Braddon than she'd thought, and somebody else must have suspected him, or known of his intentions, and had sent the moquette to the police because it constituted a clue . . . in some way or other. She pictured herself being pushed off a cliff by Tom, her last sight that of his charming, bashful smile.

And that smile had now fled. Naturally he was put out by her rejection of his proposal. Or was there another reason? Alarming sounds were coming from the glass office; it was a different coughing this time – more desperate. Tom filled a tumbler with water at the stone sink and took it to the inner office which he entered without knocking. The coughing stopped soon after. May thought she heard Tom's solicitous, low voice.

'Emphysema,' said Alec from the opposite corner of the room.

Tom returned to his desk with the pipe Williams had been smoking and put it in his desk drawer. 'Confiscated it. I do that periodically. The old boy's going to be fine. He'll sleep a little while in his chair. He always gets a little cranky on production day, and that brings on the cough.' He moved his hands through his hair. He looked pale and tired himself, but not remotely like a murderer, and May felt ashamed of herself for ever having thought he could be.

The facts, as opposed to her wild speculations, all indicated that he was a very kind man – had been right from the off when he had bought her two drinks, and it seemed perfectly clear that he had tried to protect her from Kenneth Cooper. He had acted chivalrously – also by not disturbing her in the aftermath. As for the motive she had ascribed to him: seeking to avenge Braddon's request for – what was it called? – copy approval. In a story it certainly would not pass muster as a motive for murder. It just did not 'stand up'. Whoever killed Rex Braddon had hated him for some much deeper reason.

'I'll see you tomorrow,' May said.

'Isle of Wight?' said Tom, gratifyingly delighted. 'Nine o'clock suit?'

'Where?'

'Under the clock at Waterloo,' he said, and he was nearly laughing. 'I've always wanted to say that. We'll buy returns for Portsmouth Harbour, and we'll need runabout tickets for the island.'

May did like the idea of running about with Tom.

As he escorted her to the stairs, they passed the glass part of Roy Williams' office, where he appeared to be sleeping. 'What does he use the coal scuttle for?' May asked Tom.

'Ashtray.'

15

It wasn't hard to find the clock. It was four-sided and dangled like a great lantern in the centre of the concourse. Not that there weren't plenty of other clocks at Waterloo, and most agreed that it was ten to nine when May took up her position beneath, equipped with a third-class return to Portsmouth Harbour and a runaround ticket for the Isle of Wight (which, rather excitingly, the clerk had asked her to sign).

She wore her Halifax hat, the only one that offered any protection against the sun, and was pleased to note that its red flower perfectly matched the Chinese Red of her lipstick, the sight of which seemed to have electrified quite a few of her fellow Tube travellers on the way to Waterloo. She also wore her pale blue linen dress with pleated skirt and her blue and red bow belt, which looked like two belts and so emphasised the slimness of her waist. The dress had long sleeves, so she didn't need her linen jacket, should the weather turn cold later, which it showed no sign of doing. There seemed no call for a jumper, but her white silk shawl with the lacy pattern and tassels was in her Gladstone bag. You ought not to take a Gladstone bag to the seaside, but the bag was the home of the moquette, and the moquette was the point of the trip.

Or was it just the nominal reason? The consensus seemed to be that both the moquette and the Isle of Wight trains were rather antiquated, but the chances of finding a match were surely minute, and how exactly would any such correlation point towards the killer of Rex Braddon? Would it be the start of a trail leading to the drunken 'primitive' painter Kenneth Cooper, or the snooty Guy Cavanagh? The odds seemed rather better that she would have an enjoyable day with Tom, whom she had eliminated from her list of suspects. This would probably not be the end of the complications between her and him, but she had satisfied herself as to his character. He was a kind man – and shy with it.

Her companions beneath the clock were other young women and men, all in holiday rig. One woman had recently been claimed by her man even though it was not yet nine. It was seven minutes *to*. In this sort of setting the words from bad romantic fiction – *Peg's Paper* sort of stuff – came to mind. She had to admit she was rather 'gone' on Tom Crosby, rather 'wrapped up' in him.

By two minutes to nine May was beginning to resent the greetings going on around her. Their casualness suggested complacency: 'Hello, kid. We're just in time for the non-stopper,' or, 'Here, take this,' as a woman brusquely handed her suitcase to her counterpart.

The words 'Portsmouth Harbour' were painted on a sort of wide plank wedged into the gate of Platform 7. There was a clock face at the end, like a toy clock. You had to move the hands yourself, and someone had set them at ten past nine, for the departure time.

At ten past nine, with the train presumably departing

beyond the gate, a guard or porter shifted the pointers to show 9.30. Evidently there were many trains to Portsmouth Harbour; at this rate there would need to be. While May had envisaged all sorts of strange behaviour on the part of Tom Crosby, she had not anticipated that he would not turn up. He had been the one to initiate the arrangement, after all.

You weren't meant to be standing still for any length of time in this great whirlpool of people. Every two minutes new ones would come up to the clock. They'd wait a couple of minutes before their lover arrived to take them away. At twenty past nine May had been under the clock for half an hour. At twenty-five past nine she stalked towards Platform 7, and felt the welling of tears.

The train was electric. She would have welcomed the privacy of a compartment, but she had boarded a crowded, bus-like carriage full of cheerful and noisy third-class holidaymakers. 'Is the Isle of Wight abroad, Dad?' 'We'll have a bit of dance tonight.' 'Our Bob was always sick on the Wight steamer, and he'd been in the navy!' Above the windows an advertisement showed a sun-tanned man in a jauntily tilted railway cap holding up a kind of scroll on which a list of towns was printed. Each town had a number alongside it. '"Better than ever", says Sunny South Sam', read the message beneath. '"You simply must go south for sunshine this year."' The numbers were temperature records. 'Ventnor on the Isle of Wight' was top. May had never heard of Ventnor.

This train smelt new: a kind of chemical smell. It was mainly green, but the moquette was blue and brown – jazzy splatters, trying too hard to be modern. The sunlit fields passing by cheered her up somewhat; a steam train went past the other way, its pompous breathy bustle somehow cheering. After the violence of its passing little cloudlets of steam settled gracefully over the fields, whose emptiness signified freedom. May was free of London for the day, and she would be free of Tom Crosby forever. He was just impossible. She would put him in a story, turn him into an imaginary person. A kind of assassination . . .

From her bag she took *Impasse*, the novel by Emma Dean. It had been waiting for her when she returned from Whitefriars Street. It wasn't very long, and she had already skimmed through it. The story concerned the various impasses experienced by the young heroine, Elizabeth Deacon, who of course shared her initials with the author. The initials of the character called Ralph Barton confirmed that he must be based on Rex Braddon. May wondered whether Emma Dean's perpetuation of real people's initials arose from lack of imagination or a desire that everyone should know who was being portrayed. Either way, Ralph Barton was indeed an arrogant artist.

He was a minor character, not one of the heroine's main impasses. There were two of those: Matthew and Hector. In the second half of the book, Elizabeth Deacon began regularly 'going to bed' with Matthew and Hector, which was quite alarming, because the tone of the first part of the book was prim and plain. Even after the lovemaking started the style remained plain: 'When Matthew and I made love, it was with the curtains open, whereas Hector preferred them closed.'

Elizabeth Deacon was the daughter of a lawyer and 'part French' – which part was not disclosed. Having grown up in Paris, she was thinking of settling in London. She lived in a cheap hotel, perpetually viewing flats, none of which were 'quite satisfactory', hence further impasses.

One flat, 'in a quiet area of London not far from South Kensington', turned out to be owned by Ralph Barton. Elizabeth had been expecting to be shown around by the letting agent, but Ralph Barton had been waiting for her. The book livened up a bit whenever Barton appeared, but Deacon's poor ear for dialogue also became evident. On meeting Barton, 'a large, dangerous-looking man', Elizabeth explained that the flat was unfurnished, whereas it had been advertised as furnished. 'But it is furnished,' Barton replied, indicating a painting propped against a wall. 'Can you not see?' He asked Elizabeth's opinion of it. 'Given that there is only one painting in the flat,' she replied, 'it ought to be a better one than that.' (She considered it 'quite a boring portrait of quite a boring-looking woman.') Barton then said, 'with a shrug', that it was his own work. 'He didn't seem bothered that I had not praised it.'

And then . . .

'Anyhow,' I said, 'I do not consider paintings to be furniture.'

'Well,' he said, 'there is also a bed. Would you care to try it out?'

'I am not in the least bit tired.'

'That is not what I meant.'

Instead of 'one or two large houses, which he could easily have afforded', Ralph Barton had many flats 'all over London, in respectable but slightly scruffy places'. Over the course of a further half dozen flat viewings she turned him down, and kept turning him down.

Nevertheless, Elizabeth became 'really quite curious' about Barton. She realised he had no real friends, except his many mistresses. He also had what he called his 'habitués'. These included his lawyer, Mr Garner, 'who got him out of scrapes, and sometimes contracts'; his agent (an unnamed woman), and a Mr Adrian North of the North Gallery, which often showed his works. They were all martyrs to his temper and largely indifferent to his work. But, as Barton said to Elizabeth, 'They do like those little pictures of the King's head that I keep giving them.'

The flats he showed her were either sparsely furnished or unfurnished. She didn't see another of his paintings in any subsequent viewing. None of Barton's works, according to Elizabeth, were retained by him. 'If he couldn't sell them, he destroyed them. He could hardly bear to look at them.'

She quizzed him about this.

'I suppose you always feel you can do better?'

'No. It's more that they are not very good.'

'How so?'

'I always find the paint kills the sketches – suffocates them.'

Elizabeth reflected on Barton's denigration of his own work:

I didn't consider him modest exactly, because that quality goes with a sweetness of temper he entirely lacked. It's true that when I called him an *affichiste*, because of all the posters he designed, he merely laughed and offered to send me a signed copy of one he had done for Imperial Chemical Industries – Dulux Paint! But few other people would have dared criticise him to his face, or even in print, as I discovered from various witnesses to his outbursts. He had been known to physically attack reviewers, and heaven help the waiter in a restaurant who brought him the wrong bottle of wine! No, Ralph Barton was not modest; he merely held himself in the same contempt he did most people.

Elizabeth seemed to have a morbid fascination with Barton, but it didn't lead to any dangerous entanglement, and three-quarters of the way through the book it fizzled out when Barton did her an unexpected kindness. He presented her with 'an elegant sketch of an elegant living room'. It turned out to be of a flat in Chelsea, available to rent from one of Barton's habitués, his lawyer Mr Garner. Elizabeth Deacon found it 'quite suitable'. 'I had always suspected Barton capable of the *beau geste*,' she concluded in her somewhat stilted, part-French way.

If Barton really was Braddon, the book gave was a slightly more sympathetic impression of him than May had gained from the West Gallery. The passages featuring him gave no clue as to who might have killed him. It was surely not Emma Dean, if Elizabeth Deacon could be taken to be her. The authorial voice seemed phlegmatic and tolerant, reminding May of the person who had first mentioned the novel to her, Lucy Palmer. Even so, perhaps May should try to locate Emma Dean. But the biography of the author on the back flap gave no clue as to where she might be found.

Putting the book back in her bag, it suddenly occurred to May that Tom might not have turned up because he *couldn't* turn up. What if he'd fallen foul of Rex Braddon's killer? Of Kenneth Cooper, say? Her thoughts were beginning to re-volve in the familiar whirl. A man on the opposite side of the gangway was smiling at her, which he ought not to be doing, since he was obviously sitting next to his wife. May took her handkerchief from her bag, dabbed it with her tongue and began wiping away the Chinese Red. The man's smile only widened.

The train rolled into a town past untidy, half-industrial scenes; in the carriage passengers stirred, bags and cases were taken down from the luggage racks, and it seemed everyone was ready to get off when the train came to a halt at a station, but nobody did, because this was only Portsmouth & Southsea and you couldn't catch a steamer to the Isle of Wight from here. The train was already moving again, as if the very brief stop had been made for form's sake only – out of politeness to Portsmouth & Southsea.

The smiling man was smiling at May still, now with a small suitcase on his knee. The train was entering a thicket of lines, with many signals converging, but they failed to check its progress to Portsmouth Harbour. On the platform May watched the smiling man talking perfectly amiably to his wife while repeatedly looking back at her (what an incredible nerve he had). But it seemed that the third glance he gave her from amid the crowd streaming towards the steamer dock was valedictory, because he and his wife were almost the only ones to ignore the signs to the steamers, diverging instead towards the exit for Portsmouth itself. Immediately the prospect of the 'Garden Isle' – as a it said on poster May had just walked past – became infinitely more inviting.

And the steamer was charming, with the air of a largeish boat pretending to be a ship. There were lifeboats and life-buoys, signs indicating a 'fore deck' and 'aft deck', and a crew dressed like naval men, but most tending to be older or younger – and friendlier – than May's idea of the standard sailor type. There was only one funnel, granted, but plenty of other white pipes were sticking up out of the deck, and when the paddlewheel began turning it made a churning noise that gave May butterflies in her stomach. Nearby on the deck, a father was explaining to his son, 'This waterway is the Solent.'

'But it *is* the sea, isn't it?' the boy demanded.

'It's the English Channel.'

'But that's the sea, isn't it?'

'Of course it is, Eric.'

And young Eric nodded to himself with satisfaction.

The Solent did rather have the air of a boating lake, though, with a variety of boats criss-crossing in the sunshine as though for the sheer fun of it. May went below decks, where there was a 'Saloon' which looked like a self-service café with wooden chairs and a 'First-Class Saloon' resem-bling a palm court restaurant with basket chairs and white cloths on the tables. In the saloon May queued for one of the neatly packaged 'takeaway' lunches – a bottle of lemonade, sandwiches (fish paste, reputedly) and an apple. She put the parcel in her bag and went back on deck, to see that the smaller, more frivolous craft had fallen away, as the steamer pursued a lonely course to the blue smudge on the horizon being pointed out by everyone as 'the Island'.

May knew that 'the Island' was really just a broken-off bit of Sussex, but she felt intrepid as she stood alone at the steamer's prow with the breeze playing havoc with her carefully shingled hair and sprays of seawater hitting her face.

'The Island' gradually resolved itself into a largely white place: white cliffs, white boats, white seafront villas. When these had all become quite distinct the steamer turned away from them, as though it hadn't liked the look of all that pretty Victoriana. But it was just that it was making its approach sideways, booming up to a great pier with a series of what seemed to May dangerous bounces, made more alarming by the way everybody had congregated on the side of the deck facing 'the Island'.

It was quite a relief to disembark, onto the most hyperactive pier May had ever seen. It was immensely long, and full of cars, trains, trams and people, some of whom had spurned all the many forms of transport available in favour of staying on the pier. There were a couple of big cafes-cum-dance halls and, even at 1 p.m. jazz music competed with the announcements.

But most of those who came off the steamer did follow the signs that read KEEP STRAIGHT ON FOR TRAINS. One, it seemed, was about to depart, since porters were chivvying people aboard; another was arriving, and neither train belonged to the Americanised jazz world of the pier entertainments. The engines were small and quaint with amusingly tall chimneys, and the one arriving made an eager panting noise like a dog. The carriages were various shades of green, with seemingly too many windows and doors and much fussy gold lettering, mainly reading 'Southern' and 'Third'.

May approached a 'Third', having gathered from many excited platform shouts that this was the train for Cowes. She stepped directly into a compartment, for there was no side corridor. This must be the antiquated nature of trains here that Roy and Tom had been talking about. May had the compartment to herself long enough to register the red and pink flowers on the moquette, which was presumably old-fashioned, but proudly so; it suited the train to a tee. She sat down by the window, and suddenly the compartment was full of children, apparently in the charge of a remarkably sanguine man. He smiled at May as he sat down, but it was not a sinister smile, and the children were delightful, each equipped with a bucket and spade and a blue knapsack, evidently full of treats that – being well-brought up – they were determined not to savour all at once, hence exclamations (rather loud, admittedly) such as, 'John, we're saving our sandwiches for the beach. Mary gets sick if she eats on the train.'

'I haven't even thought about food, Sarah. I'm going to read my comic.'

'I've already finished my comic. I think I'll start on my book.'

'Louise and I are just going to look out of the window for a while, aren't we, Louise?'

May was quite surprised that this civilised lot weren't in first-class.

Below the luggage rack was a framed map of the island. May had not troubled to buy a guide to the Isle of Wight, thinking Tom would know his way about, so she studied it. The island was shaped like a teapot pointing left. Cowes was at the top of the lid. Ryde was at the top of the handle. Towards the tip of the spout were Yarmouth and Freshwater. At the base of the teapot was Ventnor.

The train was rolling along the pier with resonant rumble. As it approached the land, scores of small brown birds scattered away across the glistening sand of the foreshore below. Then it stopped at the station for Ryde.

'I'm glad we're off the pier,' said the boy called John. 'I kept thinking the planks would break. I didn't want to say anything, because I would only have scared Louise' – at which one of the girls put her tongue out at him. May was relieved to observe this lapse in decorum.

After Ryde the 'Garden Isle' began living up to its name: orange wildflowers by the trackside, pretty green meadows inhabited by a few light brown cows or the occasional phlegmatic horse. The small stations looked like their names: Smallbrook Junction, Haven Street. They had picket fences and hanging baskets overflowing with flowers.

The train came to Newport: an industrial town, albeit small and sunny and on the banks of a river. Here, on a whim, May alighted, rather than continuing on to Cowes. Well, not quite a whim. She had seen more elderly-looking carriages on the opposite platform. This train was empty, apparently sleeping in the sun. She approached it and began examining all the moquettes through the windows. Afterwards she was only able to recall one of the designs – the only geometric motif amid a jumble of flowery ones: it showed dark green, fan-like shapes on a greyish background. It was quite sombre – a shadow on a sunny day.

She sat down on a platform bench to eat her packed lunch. It was rather delicious, and while the lemonade was warm the bottle was delightfully small and squarish. She tried not to imagine Tom Crosby eating his own lunch beside her, and soon found herself having to fend off negative thoughts about all her endeavours, whether this moquette quest, her writing or her apparent inability to make a 'go' of living in London.

On the platform around her, chattering people were starting to appear, a lot of them evidently from Yorkshire, which was heartening. 'It's a right suntrap is Ventnor,' she heard one woman say. The train was also waking up. All the carriages had just been rudely bumped backwards by one of the small engines, which it seemed was presuming to take them to Ventnor – 'Ventnor West!' according to the languid shouts of a porter strolling along the platform.

May would go to Ventnor. She had resolved to as soon as she'd heard the word 'suntrap'. 'Her' moquette was somewhat sun-faded, Fred Bailey of Halifax had told her. Perhaps at Ventnor there would be whole sidings of ancient trains basking in the sun? There would presumably be no *shortage* of trains, since if there was a Ventnor West station there must also be a Ventnor East.

May watched to see which compartment the suntrap woman got into. It might be useful to quiz – in a practical Yorkshire way – a female equivalent of Fred Bailey. The woman was quite large (albeit handsome with it), and distinctive by virtue of her blue dress with a white nautical motif of sailing ships and pennants connected by knotted ropes. She was obviously popular too, because several other, quieter women had followed her into the compartment, leaving no room for May. She climbed into the next one along, where she was joined by two elderly gents from the Yorkshire party.

'How do?' said the first.

The second was more voluble. 'Going along all right?'

May decided to give him a Yorkshire answer. 'Gradely, thanks,' but he only nodded, as though this were exactly the reply, and the accent, he had been expecting. Once the train had pulled away he dozed off and began to snore. His pal, embarrassed, prodded him, and the snore continued in a lower register.

The gentle snore suited the passing scene: old-fashioned corn stooks in the fields, carts top-heavy with hay, but nothing as strenuous as haymaking actually underway. Every few minutes there'd be a cottage, usually smothered by thatch. They came to a station, the platform deeply shadowed by a canopy, and as the train paused May heard the voice of the 'suntrap' woman. 'Our Bill was a cyclist, and he always said if you take your bike to Ventnor, you must have at least four gears.' As the train set off again she was drowned out not so much by the chuffing of the engine as the creaking of the old wooden carriages.

At the next station, which had no canopy and a porter mopping his brow with a handkerchief, May heard the woman again. 'Our Bill always has a drop of whisky with his cocoa at night. He used to say, "It can't do any harm and if it does, I don't care."'

May was getting a bit sick of hearing about this 'Bill'. But at the next halt, where the train was clean ignored by a porter sitting on a bench reading a newspaper, the woman came up with the goods. 'Bill just adored Ventnor. We must have been a dozen times, and it never let us down. We'd usually take one of the camping coaches on the Undercliff – lovely little spot down near Steephill Cove.'

The train went into a long tunnel. It emerged thrillingly above the dazzling sea, which it tracked all the way to Ventnor West Station, a pleasant but somewhat bathetic spot, reminiscent of a large, detached holiday villa. At the ticket gate May found herself behind the suntrap woman. 'It's the regatta today,' she was saying. 'Bill loved that. "Any excuse", he used to say, "for doing nowt but staring at the sea."' Of course, Bill must be dead. May felt sympathy as well as gratitude towards the woman.

In the small, hot and crowded station hall, lined with depictions of the Garden Isle, May went up to her. 'Excuse me – do you know where I'd find the Undercliff?'

'It's under the cliff, dear!' said the woman, and she proceeded to give detailed directions while her friends looked on admiring. In truth, the detail was unnecessary, because the gist was: go down to the front and turn right.

'Thanks ever so much,' said May. 'I love your dress, by the way.'

'Well, I love *yours*, dear,' said the woman, and she appealed to her friends: 'Looks a picture, doesn't she?' They all agreed. *Well, they would do, wouldn't they?* thought May as she headed towards the town along a treelined street called Park Avenue, whose houses looked much like the railway station. At the end the sea came into view, perhaps half a mile below, a great expanse of shining silver. It seemed – from the sudden shriek of a steam whistle – that another railway station was also near at hand. May would have a look before descending to the front.

This station was just plain 'Ventnor'. The name was proclaimed in white on a green board mounted rather clumsily on a veranda roof, with a jumble of low, wooden buildings behind. It looked like a town in the Wild West, an impression increased by the presence of two white horses in an adjacent compound, and the great chalk cliff towering over the scene. The trains, it seemed, came in from a tunnel in the cliff and entered a complicated, but just then quiet, array of tracks and platforms. There stood at one of the platforms a train without an engine; an engine without a train stood at another. *Those two ought to be introduced*, thought May, and no doubt they soon would be. Wisps of steam came from the engine. May showed her Runabout ticket to a thin, rather dazed man at the gate, walked the length of the train without an engine, then looked through the carriage windows. No sign of 'her' moquette; just the usual range of chintzy compartments. 'I'm looking for a carriage with a certain sort of seat moquette,' she said, back at the ticket gate. 'Mainly yellow.'

The man frowned for a while. 'Why?'

'It's a long story. Does anything come to mind?'

A dreamy expression overcame the man. 'You know, I *have* seen a carriage with yellow seats. Just can't think *where*, though.' May headed down into the heart of Ventnor with redoubled purpose.

The town was a sort of vertical Harrogate: attractive white Regency-period houses with fancy balconies all piled on top of one another. They all faced the sea, of course, and today the line of sailing ships that formed the regatta. There were a couple of steamers out there as well. May was descending a very sheer high street, with jolly shops, colourful cafes and fancy streetlights bent over at the top as if the lamps were hanging fruit. Even a hardware store was hung with bunting.

The tide was out, exposing a glorious sweep of red and white, because the beach was largely red (but with some white shingle attractively scattered) and crowded with white deckchairs, each one topped off with a neat rectangular sunshade. So these appeared to be special deckchairs for an especially sunny place. Ventnor looked to May like 'abroad', not that she'd ever been abroad – accustomed to sun, in other words. On the prom people were managing to look respectable in very few clothes; ice creams were being eaten with the aid of serviettes. From beneath the cafés' canopies came the tinkle of cutlery and china. The sound of a distant brass band floated on the air, perhaps emanating from the neat pier flanking the beach.

She turned right, heading west, at first on a macadamed track past putting greens, open air cafés and paddling pools. Soon it became loose white stones, and nature took over. Most of the time May was walking below shelves of white rock, which sometimes became cliffs; sometimes the path meandered near the sea, held back by stone embankments and radiating a brackish smell – and in the water, she saw large fish gliding as serenely as airships. It was as if she were part of a moving diorama – the way the different elements moved at different speeds. May was walking faster than the occasional invalids she overtook (Ventnor, it appeared, was a

165

health resort), but slower than the butterflies wobbling past her head; she was much slower than the cloud shadows flowing over the grassy banks. There must be a subtle westerly breeze amid the heat of the afternoon.

After about a mile, at the foot of a field full of daisies, she came to two camping coaches. A couple sat on deck chairs outside the nearest. The man was drinking beer from a bottle; the woman was knitting, and they were playing a record on a wind-up gramophone: dance band music. May knew about camping coaches; you'd see them intermittently beside the railway from Whitby to Scarborough: they were carriages in retirement, a reminder of the previous generation of trains. Some were more firmly rooted to the spot than others, with plumbing, perhaps, and electricity. The two in this field were not very near a railway – although just as she was thinking that May heard the whistle of an engine from the headland above. It must be the line she herself had come in on. She saw only steam descending through the sky: it would dissolve before it reached the sea. The coaches in this field must have been brought by lorry; that they were small enough to fit on a long road trailer confirmed their antiquity. Not the previous generation of trains so much as the one before.

The woman rose from her seat, picked up a bucket and moved it behind the carriage out of May's sightline. The man stowed his bottle of beer under his seat. May felt guilt for imposing on them – and for the lie she was about to tell.

'I'm so sorry to bother you. But I'm thinking of renting one of these coaches. Might I have a quick look inside – just through the window?'

The woman looked at her husband, who nodded.

'Lovely spot, isn't it?' said May.

'It is,' said the woman. There would be no conversation here. Behind May, the man lifted the needle from the record.

This carriage, like the other one, was painted a reddish brown. On each of the four doors the word 'Third' was written in gold, and there was a badge comprising the words 'London Brighton & South Coast Railway' on a blue circle, with a gold number, 431, painted inside it. Roy Williams had spoken of four- and six-wheelers, but the wheels of these carriages had been removed, which meant if May shaded her eyes she could see through the windows. The interior no longer corresponded to the four doors – there were no compartments and no railway seats. It was like an ordinary living room, with sofa and armchairs and a sort of kitchenette at the end. May said, 'Is the other carriage . . . ?'

'Just the same, yes. The people who have that one are down at the beach. They're friends of ours.'

'It's very nice, but are there any others around here?'

The question obviously suited the woman; it gave her a chance to get rid of May. 'There's one more', she said, 'three fields along. I think it's just arrived.'

May thanked her and returned to the coast path. Three fields brought her to one that met her definition of a meadow. It was lulled by the sea waves, plumped up like a cushion, and its smooth grass seemed to benefit from its own special sunbeams. In it was a black horse and a railway carriage, apparently unattended. Like the previous two it was short, venerable, without wheels and painted brown; there was the LBSCR badge again. The number this time was 652, and the gold words on the doors read 'First'. May couldn't see inside: at every window a black blind was pulled down. She had been told more than once that 'her' moquette had a certain swank, a first-class air about it, and she had always suspected it would be hard to find, elusive. *Here it is*, the drawn blinds seemed to say. She tried the handle of a door, which opened – and she was *right*.

This carriage presumably awaited its evisceration. For now, it remained a railway carriage, albeit exiled from the railway. And here, in one of its compartments, in fusty-smelling summer gloom, was her moquette: in its natural setting, sprawling over the three wide, luxurious seats on either side.

'Found you at last!' she said (and May very rarely spoke to herself). She felt like the man who found Tutankhamen's tomb, and she wanted someone with whom to share this miraculous revelation, but there was only the grazing horse.

The moquette was not far from pristine, its yellowness immediately contradicted by the black 'trellis', the mysterious blue flowers confusing the issue – or adding to the fascination . . . No wonder it had never become widespread. It was too extravagant, too decadent and strange to be sat on for years by dowdy commuters – and too vulnerable. It would show the dirt. The manufacturers must have known this, because the yellow had not been applied to the armrests, which must brave all those greasy palms; the purple-blue had been used for that. That there was no sign of dirt must be a function of scant use. This moquette had never become established, had flared only briefly, like a lightning flash.

Only now did it occur to May that the material was intact. Nothing had been cut out. She closed the door; it was odd to make that familiar railway *clunk* in an empty field. She tried the next compartment: same story. It was in the third one that she found the hole, if such a neat, rectangular excision could be so described. It was on the middle seat on the right. She stepped inside. Above the seats were photographic views of Brighton: West Pier, Boating Lake, Hotel Metropole. The floor was carpeted in grey. No footprints.

She sat down on the seat opposite the one with the hole in it. That was what you were meant to do with moquette, after all: sit on it, not chop it up. Where the moquette had been removed, horsehair bristled. But this was not pure vandalism. There was some higher purpose behind the removal: the revelation of a killer. But by what connection? Having reached the source of the mystery, May was no nearer solving it. The next task was to find out who had designed this moquette for the Brighton company – at least now she could supply a carriage number. But it felt very much like going back to square one. And next week she was back at work; she also had stories to write and a city to conquer.

'*Got* you.' A man was outside the carriage door with a shotgun under his arm. The gun was 'broken', if that was the right term: not in the shooting position. He looked like the farmer he probably was: healthily sunburned, his face about the same colour as his red neckerchief, his regular features offset by a shapeless hat. 'You're coming up to the house with me.' There was a half-smile on his lips. 'Then we'll telephone to the police. They'll be here in no time.' 'He*rrre*,' he had said – a rural accent; you were very conscious of the r's.

May was breathing fast. Therefore she ought to speak slowly. 'That's absolutely fine,' she said, 'since it's a police matter that's brought me here.' She was rather proud of that sentence, in the circumstances.

'You're lying through your teeth,' said the man, still half-smiling. 'You cut a piece out of that seat – or some friend of yours. Now you've come back for more and I've caught you.'

May shook her head. 'I'm not a criminal. I'm *investigating* a crime, and I can prove it. But I need to get something out of my bag.'

'Go ahead,' he said, which was promising, but then he closed the shotgun, which was not. He wasn't actually pointing the barrel at May, but her hands were shaking as she fished for her purse. It was important the man see Price's card before he saw the moquette. The moquette without the card would only seem to confirm her guilt.

The man gazed at the card as May began to tell her story. Soon the man 'broke' the gun again, so she knew she'd be all right, especially when the horse ambled over and seemed to be listening.

Now she produced the moquette. 'Do you want to speak to Sergeant Price?'

'Not overly.'

'He might help you find whoever cut this out. When did it happen, by the way?'

'Early June, middle of the night – about a month after we got the carriage. We've another two do pretty well, so we thought we'd get a third. There's a bloke in the works at Eastleigh who sold them. Southern Railway. Mr Sanderson. They're dirt cheap – all about fifty years old. The plan was to get this one converted for this summer, but it'll have to be next. Just haven't had the time.'

'You said he *sold* them. Does he not any longer?'

The man shook his head. 'Emigrated to Australia. Emigrated or retired, or both. Selling that thing to me was the last bit of work he did for the Southern. He'll be on the boat as we speak.' He looked out to the Channel as though expecting to see it passing.

'I don't suppose he said there was anything special about the material?' (She had guessed the man would not be familiar with the word 'moquette'.)

'He said it *was* considered a bit special. Most of them are off-the-peg patterns, sort of thing. But this was designed especially for the old Brighton railway, and for the Brighton line.'

The horse had wandered off in search of more dandelions.

'Did he say who designed it?'

'Somebody who'd been at art college.'

'Man or woman?'

'Couldn't say. I mean, *he* didn't say.' He was looking thoughtfully at the moquette. 'Nice enough pattern, ain't it?'

'Don't suppose you've ever heard of Rex Braddon?'

The man shook his head. 'What's your next move, then, miss?'

'I'm thinking of giving up. In fact – do you want my moquette? I mean *yours*. *This*. You could stitch it back into place?'

'No point doing that. We'll be taking the seats out, won't we?'

'Oh. Of course.'

'Looks like you're stuck with it, miss.' He touched his shapeless hat, giving the horse a pat on his way off.

In the still-bright evening a string of lights had been lit along the prom: reds, greens and blues, not yet coming into their own. The beach had thinned out, and the sea was now burnished rather than polished. Halfway up the high street May noticed that the shop she'd thought on the way down sold stationery was in fact a cut above that: an art shop, selling oil paints, easels and so on. Also actual art: famous and unfamous works reproduced on postcards and posters. There were original artworks, too, and a noticeboard giving details of talks and exhibitions. Walking over to it, she saw a familiar name. On 7 June Guy Cavendish had given a talk at the Ryde Literary and Scientific Institute about 'Perspectives on the Lithography of Blake'. The man who'd stalked out of the West Gallery private view . . .

Ryde was on the opposite side of the island, and his talk had been about a month before the piece of moquette had been removed. But he might have seen it in situ. Had he then come back to cut it out? And if so, *why*? Why had anyone?

A telegram was waiting on May's doormat. It was from Tom Crosby:

VERY SORRY FOR NO-SHOW (STOP) WILL
EXPLAIN (STOP) CAN YOU BEAR TO BE UNDER
ANOTHER STATION CLOCK TOMORROW. AT TEN
THIS TIME? PLATFORM ONE PADDINGTON
(STOP) HAVE FIXED UP INTERVIEW WITH
CAVANAGH AT OXFORD.

So Guy Cavanagh had come into the picture for Tom too. That was May's first thought. The second was that this telegram must have been very expensive. Yes, there was the economical and presumably American phrase, 'no-show', but even the hyphen would have cost. It was generally wordy: the work of a man with a literary sort of mind, and one keen to atone for that 'no-show'.

Of course, May was intrigued at the prospect of hearing from the supposedly stand-offish Cavanagh, and curious to know how Tom had persuaded him to a meeting. So yes, she would be under the Paddington clock at ten, but she would be somewhat reserved. Her Isle of Wight outfit would do. Minus the Chinese Red.

16

Paddington Station was as full of sunlight as its sooty glass roof allowed.

Platform 1 was packed with people waiting to board a long train that was being brought in. They were equipped for vigorous activity, with fishing rods, guns, bikes and those articles used for surf-riding that May didn't know the name of. But there was also a more pleasingly languid figure: Tom Crosby, smoking and reading the *Daily Express* under the clock that projected from the wall. All the day's other papers, it seemed, were in the rumpled canvas bag at his feet. 'Hi, May,' he said, shoving the *Express* into his bag, which gave him something to do instead of shaking her hand or kissing her. May thought he might have wanted to do the latter, if he'd known how to go about it. 'It's great to see you,' he said. 'I'm so sorry about yesterday.'

'What was the trouble?'

'Roy. I always thought his difficulty was getting *up* the stairs to our office, but on Wednesday evening he fell *down* them. Then he had a heart attack.'

'That's terrible. Is he——?'

'He's going to be OK. It was a small heart attack, apparently.'

'But the fall——?'

'Concussion and a broken arm. In the hospital he was quite distressed, so I sat with him most of yesterday. I knew he was on the mend when he started going on about dieselisation in France.'

'That's good,' said May. Was Tom someone who just kept being in the wrong place at the wrong time – or was he, after all, a murderer? Had he pushed Roy Williams down the stairs just as he might have shot Rex Braddon? With Williams he would have had a marginally better motive: take over the magazine. But it was such a small magazine. No, the notion was ridiculous, and trounced by the memory of Tom taking the glass of water through to Williams and confiscating his pipe. She was reassured by the thought that Tom's row with Braddon had occurred at the beginning of July, both by his account and Williams'. The moquette had been cut out of the Isle of Wight carriage in early June. There couldn't possibly be any connection between those events.

'The Oxford train's at quarter past,' Tom said, picking up his bag. 'Platform Three.' They set off for the booking office. 'Did you go to the Isle of Wight, May?'

She nodded.

'I think you found out something,' he said, smiling as they bought their tickets. Tom seemed to be the only man in Paddington Station not wearing a hat, and he was one of very few not wearing a jumper tucked into his trousers.

'What makes you think that?'

'You seem to be keeping something back – waiting for the right moment to tell it.'

In the dusty carriage corridor they breathed in to let

impatient people past. 'I did find something out,' said May as they stepped into an empty compartment the impatient people had spurned – perhaps because it was a 'smoker'. The moquette was undistinguished. May sat down near the window; Tom sat opposite her and offered her a cigarette, which she refused.

The train emerged from under the station roof into scruffy west London, which seemed embarrassed by the intensity of the light raying down on it. 'So lay it on me, May!' said Tom, blowing smoke sideways. He seemed to think that the more American he was, the more charming he was – and he was right.

'I *will* have a cigarette, actually,' said May, and she launched into the story first of her trip to Halifax, then of yesterday on the Isle of Wight. Tom made only occasional, railway-oriented interjections. When she referred to the carriages in the meadow as 'brown' he corrected her: 'Umber'. Her punchline, so to speak, was the revelation that Guy Cavanagh had been on the Isle of Wight at about the time the moquette was taken.

After they'd discussed the possible implications, May asked Tom how he'd persuaded Cavanagh to see them. It turned out that Tom had telephoned him yesterday after it became apparent that Roy Williams was going to be all right.

'I kind of know him,' said Tom, 'from the university.'

'Hold on. I just *knew* you went to Oxford.'

'You don't say?'

'Something about the floppy hair and white linen suits.'

'Right. Not my towering intellect. Dad wanted me at Oxford, then he *didn't* want me there.'

'Why not?'

'Got tired of subbing me, I guess. You ever read an Ernest Hemingway novel, *The Sun Also Rises*?'

May had not.

'Bill asks Mike, "How did you go bankrupt?" "Two ways", says Mike: "Gradually, then suddenly." With Dad, that second stage occurred when I was at Oxford. He pulled the plug at the end of my second year.'

'So you don't have a degree?'

'Nope. What I do have is a diploma in journalism from London University, which I signed up for immediately after.'

'And who paid for that?' May asked, rather rudely.

'Me, funnily enough, with the proceeds of freelance writing and tutoring. It was my declaration of independence from Dad.'

'So that's what journalism means to you? Independence?'

'It can also be fun.'

'Even on the *Railway Digest*?'

'No, not there. But let's finish up about Cavanagh. We were at the same college.'

'Which one?'

'Merton.'

'Never heard of it,' said May. 'It's not one of the famous ones.'

'No,' said Tom, perhaps a little dashed. 'But it's about the oldest. I'd talk a bit to Guy in the dinner queue. I think he found me an interesting curiosity.'

'Why?'

'Because I hadn't been to Eton, or somewhere like that.'

'Where *did* you go to school?'

'Lot of places, some of which I've actually forgotten.'

'You moved around a lot?'

'Dad did, so mother and I did too.'

'Is your mother still alive?'

'Yep. Not with Dad, though. Lives in Italy.' He sat back, smoking. His hair was in his eyes. He brushed it out of his eyes. As she looked at him he smiled. They were passing fields now. Sunbeams kept flashing in through the window. 'What say you and I, May – I mean, how about if . . .'

'Yes?'

'—We swing by Merton?'

May had been rather hoping for Italy.

'I'll show you the Fellows' Garden. You'll like it. We're a little ahead of time for seeing Cavanagh.'

'Sure,' she said, which was an American sort of answer, she thought. Tom seemed to like it, anyhow.

Walking to Merton College they passed other colleges, or at least their forbidding double front doors, some tantalisingly open and usually disclosing a well-kept lawn, as if the grass was the hallowed thing that must be guarded. They stepped away from the High Street ('the High', Tom called it) into a quiet square where there was a back entrance to a big college and a front entrance to a smaller one. The next street was even quieter, cobbled and slightly kinked with a few tall, ancient trees, as if to prove how wrong-headed the builders of all other streets had been.

The man at the Merton gate knew Tom. He called him 'sir'; Tom called him 'Bill'. The front quadrangle echoed to the sound of birdsong, so you knew the garden wasn't far

178

off. The Fellows' Garden was surrounded by a beautiful old wall, like a medieval city wall, with flowers growing on a bank below. A few people sprawled on the grass, supposedly reading but usually talking and smoking.

'It must have been a wrench to leave here,' said May.

'Uh-huh.' Tom pointed at a stone seat on the bank. 'I have recollections of Guy Cavanagh sitting there and sketching, always alone.'

'You did well to persuade him to see us.'

'He'll *see* us, May. That's his code of honour. How much he says will be another matter. I'm quite sure he doesn't know who killed Rex Braddon, and if he *does* happen to know . . .'

'He might not want to say?'

Tom nodded slowly.

May asked Tom whether he knew that Cavanagh had considered becoming a priest.

'I did not, but it's not completely surprising, May.'

On that same stone seat they ate the sandwiches and drank the lemonade they had bought at the station. Tom asked her about her own school, so May told him about Princess Mary's, which naturally led on to her friendship with Ellie, with a particular focus on their experience at the West Gallery. May felt the mystery between herself and Tom falling away at a faster rate than the mystery of the moquette.

17

They entered the Ashmolean Museum at three o'clock behind a trickle of tourists. The Drawing School was on the first floor; it looked like an exhibition hall that had been cleared of exhibits: a grand, high-ceilinged place with tall windows and small, disparate desks like forms from various schools. The room's only occupant was a janitorial figure who may or may not have given May and Tom a nod of greeting from the distant table where he was noisily cranking a pencil sharpener. Occasionally he'd blow on a pencil tip, again noisily – or it might just have been the room's acoustic, which was now exaggerating the sound of fast-approaching footsteps. In walked Guy Cavanagh. With his bony, patrician features and curly hair he looked like one of the classical statues from another room come to life. 'Hello, Tom, it's nice to see you. And this is——?'

Before Tom could reply, Cavanagh called over to the janitor, whose loud grinding of the pencils had not abated. 'Todd! Is it really necessary to do that?'

The man did not stop cranking straight away. When he did he said, 'There's a class at four.'

'Yes, and it's an art class, not engineering drawing.'

The man blew on the pencil he'd just sharpened, which was the next most insubordinate thing to starting on a new pencil, May thought. 'Have I to put out the casts, then?' he said.

'If you can do it quietly.'

The man marched out through a door at the far end.

'This is May,' said Tom. 'I told you about her on the phone.'

'Of course. May.' May felt Cavanagh was weighing up her name and finding it somehow lacking. They shook hands, and he turned back towards Tom. 'What are you up to these days, Tom? I don't think you said?'

'After I went down, I did a course in journalism.'

Unexpectedly Cavanagh turned towards May, almost, if not quite, smiling. 'He was *always* doing a course on journalism, this fellow. Appropriated all the papers in the JCR every morning. He actually *read* the *Daily Express*, if you can believe it?'

So May was to be included after all. She felt that Cavendish, not wanting to have the conversation that was clearly in the offing, had made a token attempt to put it off, only to realise this was a futile endeavour. His question had been by way of apology – not that any answer was required. 'You have your piece of moquette?' he said, indicating the bag. 'Apparently a policeman gave it to you?'

May felt like a child known to be foolishly proud of some trinket. When she produced the moquette Cavanagh gave a quick nod, which May took to be reluctant recognition.

In recapping the tale, with supporting comments from Tom, she watched Cavanagh closely as she said the words 'Isle of Wight', but could see no particular reaction. Having told the basic tale, May and Tom had returned to the suspicious nocturnal activities of Kenneth Cooper when the man Todd reappeared, wheeling a squeaking barrow loaded with plaster busts.

Cavanagh winced theatrically. 'Todd,' he said, 'take that away at once.'

'But you said—'

'We are now having a private conversation. Come back when we're gone.'

Todd departed again slowly, muttering something possibly along the lines of 'That would be a pleasure'.

'Cooper?' said Cavanagh. 'I think he's out of the picture. He's a sot, not a killer. He was one of the few people somewhat indebted to Braddon. Braddon was his patron for a while.'

'But Braddon had an affair with his wife,' said May.

'*Did* he? I didn't know that.'

'But it doesn't surprise you, right?' said Tom.

'Absolutely not.'

'He didn't like it when I produced the moquette,' said May. 'But that might just have been because he heard the word "police".'

'Well, that makes sense, in light of what you say about the affair. He would have known he might be considered a suspect.'

'This seemed to mean something to you, as well,' May said, looking from the moquette to Cavanagh.

Cavanagh hesitated. Then he seemed to make a decision. 'In its design roughly, and in its colour precisely, it reminds me of a series of marbled papers that a colleague of mine produced about twenty years ago, just after the War. Do you know about marbling?'

'We know books have marbled end papers,' said Tom, and May rather liked that 'we'.

'You thicken water,' said Cavanagh, 'usually with stuff called carrageenan, which is a sort of seaweed essence. You drop paint or ink into it and swirl it into what you consider an attractive design. Then you lay a paper treated with alum on the water and it takes on the pattern. My colleague put a lot of yellow in the water, a colour he was obsessed with; he offset it with purply circles, with a drop of black in the middle. These were the colours of flowers he had – in large number – in his garden.'

'But what about the trellis effect?' said May. 'The black diamonds?'

'I'm coming to that,' Cavanagh said, a bit irritated. 'My colleague played with this motif and these colours many times. He had a workshop in town, on the edge of Port Meadow, not far from here. I'd go there with him sometimes and he showed me the results, which were never quite what he saw in his head, apparently. One day, in my presence, he painted that trellis effect, as you call it, over the top. He was sort of crossing the whole thing out, but I rather liked the result. I told him so, and he obviously came around to it himself, because after that the black lines became a fixture. He began to paint the design repeatedly, always modifying it a little. The yellow became stronger; the purple-blue shape he reined in slightly. It became less spiky, more rounded. The whole motif meant something to him philosophically, especially the yellow with the black on top: the contradiction of life.'

'And the design found its way onto a moquette?' said May.

'So it appears. Unless this is the most remarkable coincidence.'

It was Tom who asked the important question. 'And who is this colleague of yours?'

'He taught drawing here with me.'

'His name?'

Cavanagh seemed to take a further decision. 'I don't mind telling you. His name's Patrick Moss, and he certainly didn't kill Braddon, at least not from what I've read of the crime. Patrick was the gentlest of souls. Of course, people invariably say that about murderers, but there can be no nipping in and out of first-storey flats for Patrick, I fear. He was a cripple from early childhood – curvature of the spine. It was degenerative, I think. He stopped working here about ten years ago, and he was becoming a bit peculiar at that point. Not in a dangerous way, I hasten to add. He was always insular, a loner, and when he taught here the students found him strange, but also very inspiring. I heard a few years back that he'd deteriorated further. Some sort of breakdown.'

'Did he ever design moquette?'

'Not as far as I know. That's applied art. You're dealing with company chairmen and so on. You need to be hard-headed to mix in that commercial world, or at least sociable – at least, *worldly*. Patrick was on the design course at the RCA, but it never really suited him. He should have been on the painting course. He was always a brilliant portraitist, and an excellent draughtsman.'

'Successful?' said Tom.

'Not at all.'

May said, 'Did Patrick Moss know Rex Braddon?'

'Did he know him?' Cavanagh sighed. 'Yes. They were on the design course together.'

He had disclosed that intelligence with particular reluctance, May thought.

'We'd like to pay him a visit,' said Tom. 'Does he still live in Oxford?'

'No', said Cavanagh. He said it rather too quickly, May thought. There was something jarring about the moment, anyhow. It was perhaps because she had spotted a movement over Cavanagh's shoulder, a slight rearrangement of shadows beyond the far door, which had remained open after Todd's exit.

'—At least, I don't think he does,' Cavanagh was saying. 'I haven't seen him for years, so I'm afraid I don't know his current address.'

'Do you think it might be on record here?' asked May.

'How do you mean?' said Cavanagh sharply.

'In the museum office.'

'You suppose they keep track of all former tutors?' Cavanagh seemed to have grown taller, to have regained the upright hauteur May had noticed when he declared at the West Gallery that Braddon had got what he deserved. May had no doubt that if he were able right now to stalk out of the room and hail a taxi as he had in Bond Street, that's just what he would have done.

In the event, he did the next best thing. 'I'm sorry,' he said, 'but I do have a class to prepare for. It's lovely to see you, Tom,' and he shook Tom's hand. Evidently it had not been quite so lovely to see May, who only merited a nod. 'I'm sorry not to have been more helpful, but I've told you all I can.'

*

'Well, I know he's your friend, and everything . . .'

May and Tom had returned to the cool, marbled lobby of the Ashmolean.

'But he was lying, right?' said Tom.

'Towards the end, anyway. He knew he had to account for his having recognised the moquette. He couldn't just shrug that off. And maybe his conscience prompted him to say as much as he did. But he couldn't bring himself to tell us where this Patrick Moss lived.'

'You think he really knows?'

'Probably. But there might be someone else who knows. Mr Todd, who was listening throughout.'

Tom nodded. 'I reckon his quarters are near the drawing school.'

'Yes, because it took him no time at all to fetch that trolley.'

'So there's a danger of bumping into Guy again.'

'I'll go; he already hates me . . .'

'He doesn't *hate* you, May.'

'. . . And Todd hates *him*, so perhaps he'll tell us whatever Cavanagh didn't want to.'

Back upstairs May had to walk past the main door of the drawing school, which stood open. Her shoes clacked horribly on the marble floor. She glimpsed Cavanagh, sitting motionless at one of the forms – recriminating with himself for having lied, perhaps, or for having withheld the important part of the truth.

Todd's door, too, was open. He was rolling a cigarette amid a jumble of brushes and buckets and dusty, discarded works of art. He smiled when he saw May. She suspected he knew exactly why she'd come. 'Hello, love,' he said. 'I think you want to get hold of a fellow used to work here? Patrick Moss?'

'Do you remember him?'

'I do.' Todd ran his tongue expertly along the length of his cigarette.

'Mr Cavanagh said he no longer lives in Oxford.'

'I know he did.'

'Is that your understanding?'

'My *understanding*, love,' said Todd, the unlit cigarette now wobbling in his lips, 'is that he never did live in Oxford, but always a little way outside.'

'Where?'

'Boar's Hill. Ever heard of it?'

'No.'

'Your pal will have. The one who was at the university.'

'Do you know *where* in Boar's Hill?'

'Now, that I don't. It's not a big place, though. You'll ferret him out, I'm sure.' He lit his cigarette and blew smoke as he smiled.

18

'What's that?' said May. The taxi had carried them past the grand colleges, golden in the sunshine, ordinary terraced houses, and now to their left there was a fine park.

'Christ Church Meadow.' Tom had taken a cigarette from his packet but not lit it, perhaps in deference to the taxi driver. Or perhaps because he'd forgotten he was holding it. A river came and went. May didn't want to ask Tom its name; he seemed to have gone distracted again.

Factories began to appear. The taxi turned left at a sign reading A420 and some word May didn't have time to read. They were in the countryside now. Tom had been quiet too long. 'If this Patrick Moss really is our man,' May said, 'you can write it all up for an article. Not for the *Railway Digest*, of course.'

'Too right,' he said. 'I'm leaving the *Digest*.'

'Oh, why?'

'Because of Roy.' He left it at that. The car was climbing, and they were approaching another sign. 'Boar's Hill.' 'If Patrick Moss *is* our man,' said Tom, 'we might have trouble on our hands.'

May had thought that, too, but she had been more worried

about Tom's silence, now thankfully broken. It occurred to her that he was the sort of person who said little when he was anxious. It was just as common as the opposite tendency. They were passing the long wall of a manor house. On the other side of the road were fields, and beyond them May saw Oxford: all the most beautiful buildings, it seemed, huddled together in a grassy hollow. Then they were running along an avenue of big white houses with flagpoles and tennis courts in their front gardens. May did not feel this was the sort of place an artist would live in. Nor, it appeared, did Tom. 'I think we need the older part,' he said, and the driver turned the car around.

The older part, it transpired, was *called* Old Boar's Hill, and here the driver let them out.

The houses were all half hidden from the chalk road May and Tom were walking along by trees or overgrown gardens, and they didn't seem to have anything as vulgar as numbers. Every so often gunshots came from some far field.

'Is it the shooting season?' May asked.

'Search me.'

'It usually is in the countryside, I think.'

No two houses looked the same, and no two faced the same direction. A leaning red telephone box was perched on a verge. Tom said, 'Shall we start knocking on doors?'

'I want to see all the gardens first,' said May.

Towards the end of the lane they came to a stone cottage. The way the front lawn billowed up to it gave the impression of it being half underground.

'That's definitely the one,' May said. 'Look at the flowerbeds.'

They were largely yellow, thanks to masses of late-flowering pansies, which also incorporated the purple-blue of the moquette. The yellow was in sunflowers as well, and in the crowds of daisies on the lawn. Tom pushed the broken gate, and the gravel path took them slightly uphill so they were looking down on a one-storey house, and here they could see that its dark blue door was ajar.

'What do we say to him?' said May.

'We say we're journalists, working on a feature about the late Rex Braddon.'

'Both of us?'

'Sure. We write under a joint byline.'

'I don't even know what that is.'

'OK, we're *researching* an article on Braddon.'

The small, shadowy hall, they could see, was dark blue and hung with dark portraits of various sizes, almost as many as the wall space allowed. All the subjects looked distorted and anxious. There was a small antique table in the hallway on which were piled ragged canvases, the topmost a painting of half a dozen incompatible-looking trees, with a far-off black house visible in a gap between them. Next to the canvases was a cracked blue and red pot bristling with paint brushes and pencils. In the shadows the blueness moved: a man had appeared. He was small and walked with a limp. He wore a torn, dark blue jumper and what might have been the trousers and boots of any farm labourer, but his head was extremely artistic, in that he looked like a pixie or a faun, with perfectly symmetrical pale features, intensely blue eyes almost too pretty for a man, and translucent, triangular ears. He seemed to take a while to notice these two people standing on his doorstep, and when he did, he said, very softly, 'Yes?'

May said, 'We're very sorry to trouble you, Mr Moss . . .' and the man nodded, as though confirming that he *was* Mr Moss.

'We're journalists,' said Tom, 'researching a feature on Rex Braddon. We believe you knew him? I suppose you heard the sad news?'

'Yes', he said. 'Well . . . how are you?' He looked dazed, as though just awoken from a long sleep.

May said, 'Might we come in?'

The little man didn't quite step aside, but it was clear he wouldn't stop them from entering the house.

The hallway seemed too small for the three of them, especially with the worried-looking people in the portraits adding to the crowd. They seemed to drift into a small stone room with a collapsing couch of red velvet. Two walls were painted black, two yellow. On one of the black walls were about 20 paintings – strange landscapes, foregrounded by beautifully coloured *lumps*, which might be rocks or trees or hills. On the black mantelpiece were trailing, dying plants. One must have had yellow flowers, since there were yellow petals on the hearth.

Tom had taken a notebook and a pen from his pocket. 'Lovely room,' he said. 'Are these paintings by you, sir?'

'Yes, but they're not for sale.'

'They're very beautiful. Might we ask you a few questions about Mr Braddon?'

'Have you got a cigarette?' said Patrick Moss.

'Sure.' Tom held out the box of *Star* brand.

As he came to take the cigarette Moss's infirmity became clearer. He rocked to the left as he walked, and in his body there was too little of the upper half.

Moss blew the smoke carefully, like a child blowing bubbles. 'I like cigarettes,' he said. 'I've been a little ill recently. My sister's looking after me. She's been very good through it all. She's coming here very soon.'

May brought the piece of moquette out of her bag. 'Do you recognise this, Mr Moss?'

He did recognise it, May was sure of that, but all he said was, 'Well, my sister's in charge, really. She's gone away to fetch something, but she'll be back soon. Excuse me, please. I must just go and see if that's her.'

There had been no sound from outside and no telephone had rung, but Patrick Moss quit the room.

'What now?' said Tom.

May said, 'I think I know who his sister is.'

Patrick Moss had returned; he was holding a small revolver. 'I would like you to leave now, please. My sister's coming and we're off away.' As he spoke he was pointing the gun at May, perhaps only because she was closer to him than Tom. But with a single pace Tom interposed himself between Moss and May, whose relief that he really was on her side outweighed her fear of the gun. But her heart was racing as she and Tom were directed out of the room and into the hallway by Moss's waving of the gun. The front door was still open. They stepped into the garden, and Moss did not follow them. Glancing back, May saw he had placed the gun on the hall table next to the pencil pot, just as though it were merely a bunch of keys.

Beyond the gate May and Tom found themselves beneath an ancient apple tree around a slight bend, the last twist of the lane. 'Who's the sister?' said Tom.

'Nancy Marshall. She's my friend Ellie's art teacher.'

'The one who didn't go to the private view?'

'That's it; because she couldn't stand Rex Braddon.'

'What makes you think it's her?'

'Slight facial similarity to her brother. When I saw her she had mud on her boots, which suggests she lives in the country. And she uses red and gold pencils, like the ones in that house.'

'We wait for her, right?'

'Yes.'

'Name's different, of course.'

'She's a widow.'

Nancy Marshall was like Mrs Henderson, May thought. She had transcended a dead husband.

'Do you think she killed Braddon?'

'Well, her brother certainly didn't.'

Tom threw down his cigarette and stood on it. He brushed his hair back and smiled. 'He's the only person in this affair who's pointed a gun at us, May. So far, anyhow.'

'His house is all on one level. I think he'd have the greatest difficulty with stairs. Braddon was shot in a first-floor flat by somebody who then ran away.'

It occurred to May that she was finally having her adventure – but in the country, not London.

A large black crow had been stalking about in the undergrowth. It was now staring fixedly at them. May kicked the air in its general direction. It did not flinch, and neither did it move at the rising note of a car engine. 'Here she comes,' said May.

By moving slightly beyond the range of the tree's branches, they could see the car. 'Jowett', said Tom. 'An old one.'

The car was black, with a dusting of white from the chalky road. The top was down, probably permanently given the crumpled looks of its folded state; the only occupant was the driver. She parked it somewhat side on, so that May could make out two suitcases and other objects roped to the grid at the rear. The engine had stopped with a very final *tick*. That the driver was Nancy Marshall was confirmed by her confident stride up the garden path. She wore the same elegant grey suit she had taught drawing in. May and Tom moved a little closer to the gatepost as Nancy entered the house. 'What's the Colt doing here?' they heard her say.

Her brother's reply was inaudible.

'With the *gun*, Patrick? Then they *know*! Where are they now?'

Inaudible reply from Patrick, but Nancy Marshall answered her own question. 'Gone to fetch the police, I'm sure. For heaven's sake, darling!'

Nancy came rocketing out of the house, gun in hand. Out of the gate, she turned left, whereas May and Tom were to her right. But the bird betrayed them. It cawed hollowly as though affronted. As it became noisily airborne Nancy turned and approached them. She held the gun a good deal more confidently than her brother.

Again Tom interposed himself, as if this were the second attempt to get some slow, formal dance going.

'Who are you and what do you mean by disturbing my brother? You have the wit to see that he's not well, I suppose?'

'Now look,' said Tom, 'we're not going to answer any questions until you stow that gun.'

'Oh yes you are.' Nancy Marshall was looking at May. 'I recognise you. You're a friend of Ellie Bancroft's. You came to the Morley to meet her.'

May's heart still raced, but the main effect the gun had on her was to focus her thoughts and her speech. 'Yes,' she said, 'and you wouldn't want to shoot a friend of Ellie's, would you?'

'I wouldn't want to shoot *Ellie*. I don't particularly want to shoot you and your friend either, but I will do if you don't tell me what you're doing here.'

May stepped sideways, out of Tom's protective shadow.

'May,' he said, 'get back.' And he took up a blocking position again.

May appreciated the gesture, but the only thing it would bring about was that Tom would be shot first. 'I want to show her the moquette,' she said to Tom. To Nancy Marshall, she said, 'I'm going to take something out of my bag. Is that all right?'

Nancy Marshall nodded. Her brother had appeared in the lane behind her. He held a large canvas holdall. May flourished the moquette once again, wondering whether this might be for the last time. 'I think this means something to you and your brother, Mrs Marshall.'

'It's the pattern he stole, Nance,' Patrick Moss said from behind his sister, who appeared to ignore him.

'I'm going to have to ask you to get in the car, I'm afraid.'

Nancy Marshall ushered them, with her brother by her side and the gun in her hand, up the lane to the car. When they reached the garden gate she said, 'You might at least shut the door, Patrick.'

Patrick did not lock the door, May noticed, merely closed it, which said to her they were either coming back soon, or never. The two suitcases attached to the back of the car suggested the latter.

'You'll sit in the back,' Nancy told them.

There were two doors for the rear seats, but only one for the front, and it was not on the driver's side. But Nancy gained the driving position with practised ease. She might be 50 years old, but had the agility of a much younger woman. Her brother threw his bag unsteadily into the footwell on the passenger side and climbed in.

Nancy pulled a button on the dashboard – must be the choke, thought May, who was paying closer attention to the driving of a car than she ever had done before. 'Point the gun at them,' Nancy told her brother. 'He'll shoot you if I tell him to,' she said, turning around, 'and possibly if I don't.'

19

They were hurtling up the lane throwing dust into a hot sky that was starting to turn pink.

'Where are we headed?' Tom said.

'A quiet place,' said Nancy without turning around.

Tom leant over and nudged May: they were passing the telephone box at the top of the lane. 'Maybe she wants to put us out in some place away from those,' he whispered.

May appreciated his positivity, and his smile.

'Mind if we smoke?' he called forward.

Nancy gave a flickering glance into the rear-view. 'If you can get it lit.' It seemed she had determined to make that impossible by the speed with which she drove past the long manor house wall, which didn't seem so long this time. The city of Oxford, sleeping in its little hollow, whirled in a quick circle. Tom put a cigarette in his mouth, lit it and passed it to May. It was like an indirect kiss. He lit another for himself. He seemed to have been lighting cigarettes in fast cars all his life.

'Can I have one, Nance?' said her brother.

'No, Pat. Just hold the gun.'

There was no expression in Patrick's eyes. He would do

what his sister said. She was everything to him. Occasionally he glanced forward, as though mildly curious as to where they might be going. Did he know?

They came to the sign that pointed back into Oxford. Nancy kept straight on, accelerating. May watched her dusty boots on the pedals, her long, elegant hand on the gear stick: she was a very good driver, better than the car deserved. They were going too fast through a big village. 'Keep the gun down a little,' Nancy instructed her brother.

A bigger sign: A40, Cheltenham to the left, London to the right. Nancy chose London, and now seemed determined to make the speedometer reach its limit: 60 miles an hour. You could tell by the scream of the engine that it didn't like being kept at that pitch.

'We're going around the top of Oxford,' Tom muttered, throwing his cigarette away. They were in a blander land-scape: petrol garages, wide, parched fields, occasional small, smokeless factories. There were few other cars on the road. Any they encountered they swung past it effortlessly. The whole world had gone on holiday.

Tom nudged May's thigh: the bag in the footwell on Patrick's side – it wasn't properly closed. A red guidebook was peeking out: *Baedeker's French Riviera*. May nodded, but Nancy had seen them noticing the book. Did she mind? Knowing the ultimate destination of their captors could not have improved May and Tom's chances of survival.

Suddenly the car sounded more relaxed at its top speed, as though it had got used to the idea, which was perhaps why Nancy began to speak. 'That piece of moquette . . .' she said. 'The design was my brother's, one of many of his stolen over the years by Braddon. If you were to walk around our house you would see, in the perspectives, compositions and colour schemes of Patrick's paintings, any number of images that have since appeared in posters for Shell Oil, Dulux Paint, the London & North Eastern Railway, the London Underground. It's not as though Braddon took pains to hide his theft; he stole as much as he liked and admitted doing so. He'd come around here with his damned box camera, for heaven's sake. "Don't mind me, old man," he'd say to Patrick. "Just doing a little research." He knew very well that that Patrick would do nothing except continue to create wonderful art, far deeper and more profound than anything Braddon was capable of.

'That moquette,' she continued, 'was his first offence, as the lawyers say. He'd watched Patrick working it up when they were both at the RCA. It was something Patrick was doing on marbled paper. Our bathroom was full of sheets of it, like so many towels drying out. He did the marbling in the bath, you see.'

Here Patrick interjected. 'When you had a bath, the water was yellow, wasn't it, Nance?'

She nodded. 'It was, darling, it was. Braddon, being a friend of Patrick's at the time – I use the term in its loosest possible sense – was often in that bathroom, being sick after drinking too much of our wine.

'Well. There was a man from the London Brighton & South Coast Railway. A sort of railway dandy. His name doesn't matter. I can hardly bear to say it, actually. He'd inherited some shares or something, and he had a say in the artistic side of things. Publicity – books and posters – and the moquettes of the carriages. He hung about the RCA in a vampiric sort of way. He took the "design" lot out to the hotel in Victoria Station. The Grosvenor, is it? Well, not all of them. Patrick didn't fancy going along. Bit too much good taste, you see.

'This . . . person happened to be looking out for moquettes just then, and of course Braddon pitched Patrick's design to him, passing it off as his own. The man appreciated its flamboyance. He commissioned Braddon, who either sent him his own painting of Patrick's pattern or possibly one of the originals he'd stolen from us.'

Just then Nancy had to attend to the road. A car she wanted to overtake kept swerving out as though to stop her.

'Lower the gun, Patrick,' she said, when they eventually went by. It would have been beneath the dignity of the overtaken driver to look their way anyhow. He simply stared sulkily ahead.

'Of course,' Nancy went on, 'this Brighton Railway man knew people who knew people. He was a big wheel in the Design and Industries Association, and the Artworkers' Guild, if you can believe it of a man who never did a day's work in his life. Well, he liked Rex Braddon, for one reason or another. He talked him up, got him work, and Braddon met most of his commissions with a steal from Patrick. And the series of landscapes he called the "Dreams" – which most people think are the only worthwhile things he ever did – are duplications of Patrick's work.

'Some people saw Braddon for the imposter he was. I think Frank Pick's in that category – but even he took a couple of things from him. Must have been in moments of distraction. Anyhow, Rex Braddon was on his way. He had arrived, and he wasn't going to depart. I would like to know how you got hold of it. The moquette.'

Tom leant over to May and whispered, 'Because *she* sent it to the cops, right?'

That was just what May had been thinking. The moquette could only have been sent for two reasons: either the sender wanted to implicate some third party, or they wanted to implicate themselves – to boast about having done the crime for a virtuous reason. May was satisfied that Nancy had shot Braddon for what she considered a moral reason. It was logical that she might want to at least give the police the chance of discovering that reason. But surely it was not quite logical to supply the clue before she had (as the writers of the crime stories had it) 'made good her escape' – and her brother's, too.

May simply had to ask the question, but first she must explain about the appearance of Sergeant Price at Quarmby & Bates's. Nancy listened without turning round or looking in the mirror, so May could not detect her reaction. She pressed on regardless. 'I assume you were the one who sent it to Scotland Yard? In a way, I suppose, you wanted them to know the truth. But wasn't it a bit reckless to send it so soon, before your escape to . . . wherever you're off to? You risked your freedom, and maybe your life. You risked your brother's freedom, too, and the whole future the two of you might have.' May looked at Patrick – and therefore at the gun. 'Patrick, did you know that Nancy sent the moquette to the police?'

Beside her Tom was shaking his head, incredulous but half smiling.

Patrick turned to his sister. 'What does she mean, Nance? What did you tell the police?'

'I told the police nothing.'

'But you not only sent them the moquette,' said May. 'You also wrote a note with it. It said, "Here's a clue to a forthcoming murder."'

'*Did* you, Nance?' Patrick's voice was weak and flat.

Nancy had stamped harder on the accelerator, and now her brother had to shout against its straining yammer. '*Did* you, Nance? Why didn't you tell me you were going to do that?'

'Of course I didn't send it. Braddon sent it.'

Tom was looking sidelong at May as though requesting permission to ask his own question. When May nodded he said, 'You're saying he sent a note to the police about his own murder a week before it happened?'

'Exactly.'

'That's pretty hard to credit,' said Tom, and that did the trick.

'He *knew* he was going to be killed,' said Nancy. 'He knew because I told him. But I did not tell the police.'

May said, 'You mean you told him *you* were going to do it?'

'Oh, for heaven's sake. Someone had to finish him off. I would see him from time to time at art events, and I would say, it's coming, you know – nemesis. It's not today, Rex, but it's not far off. He would laugh, but he knew. The last time I saw him – well, the time before last – I happened to run into him in Hyde Park. I'd just found out, rather belatedly, that he'd been appointed an RA, a Fellow of the Royal Academy. I said, I really don't think you'll have more than a few days to enjoy that little ego boost.'

Here was her confession – near enough, at any rate – and her brother didn't seem to mind, because she wasn't disclosing anything that hadn't been planned between them, and it was clearly the truth. May knew, from her reading of *Impasse*, that Braddon was fatalistic; he perhaps *hoped* for nemesis to strike. It would be a necessary corrective, and he was a game-player with a black humour. It would be against his code to 'split' on Nancy Marshall. That would be unmanly and undignified, and in any case what evidence did he have that she had made her threats? So he would lay a trail, see if anyone was clever enough to follow it after his death. He would go to the Isle of Wight and cut out a piece of the moquette that signified the start of his career.

Nancy had braked slightly behind a slower car driven by a man who was looking at the roadside fields as much as the road ahead. But now she saw an opportunity, even though another oncoming car was rapidly approaching. 'Gun,' she whispered to her brother. Patrick lowered the revolver again, and in the instant available to her Nancy swerved out and in. The other car hadn't liked it – its bulb horn quacked in protest – but the move had been beautifully done. *If I'm to die this evening,* May thought, *it won't be in this car.*

Nancy, her voice perfectly even despite what had just occurred, said, 'Let's say somebody *else* did it. Do you think Patrick and I would stay around to be questioned? A lot of people hated Braddon, but nobody more than me, and nobody with more reason that Patrick.' She removed her left hand from the wheel in order to touch her brother's shoulder. 'I know *you* didn't hate him, darling, but that's only because you're some sort of angel.'

Now they were slowing, turning off the A40; a sign said 'B482', and they were accelerating again. Evening country scenes flickered by: a cricket match being wound up, people carrying drinks into a pub's front garden. At a sign reading 'Fingest' they turned off onto a smaller road, and were going down a steep hill, practically *falling* down it. A word came to May: 'headlong'. There were trees on either side. Beams of low sun and shadows of branches rolled over the car.

Patrick turned to his sister. 'It'd be good to paint those birches just now. The trunks look like peeling paint in an old house. They don't belong outside, I think. Do you see what I mean, Nance?'

'I do, darling, I do. There'll be plenty of time for painting soon enough.'

They were amid denser trees now, the shadows continuous. The car skidded to a stop.

'What are we going do now?' Patrick asked his sister with no great urgency.

'Give me the gun, darling, and get out of the car. We're going to take them into the woods.' She waved the gun for May and Tom to get out.

Tom's sardonic smile had disappeared, and May felt a much greater fear of the gun now that all the incidental questions about Braddon's murder and the sending of the moquette had fallen away.

'Why are we taking them into the woods?' What bothered May was the note of alarm in Patrick's voice.

Nancy gave the answer to May and Tom. 'My brother's going to tie you up.'

It was as though May had just been given a present: another 60 years of life at least.

Patrick looked at his sister. 'There's spare rope on the grid,' she said

Patrick Moss might be a slow walker, but an artist of his skill had to be manually accomplished, and his ropework was efficient. He placed May and Tom either side of a sycamore tree, their backs to the trunk and their bags by their feet. He tied May's left wrist to Tom's right, and vice versa. When the job was done, he turned to his sister. 'Shall we say sorry to them, Nance?'

'*You* can if you want.'

But Patrick wouldn't act independently of Nancy, so there was no apology.

When Nancy and Patrick were back at the car, Tom called over, 'Other people might be tried and convicted for what you did. Have you thought of that? Why not set the record straight?'

Nancy seemed to think about this, but not for long. 'I don't believe the police have any evidence against anyone.' For the first time there was perhaps a hint of amusement in her eyes.

20

'You OK, May?'

It was strange to converse with someone while facing in the opposite direction, and she couldn't shuffle around to him unless he shuffled away from her. 'Of course, we know where they've gone,' she said. 'Or where they're trying to get to.'

'Boat train for Paris. Leaves Victoria at half past nine. It's now . . .'

By the pressure of the rope on her left wrist May could tell he was trying to peer at his watch.

'. . . Quarter past seven.'

'Will they make it?'

'They've a fair chance. Of course, they'll have to ditch the gun – and the car.'

'Did you see they had two paintings on the back?'

'Two paintings and two bags. I could use a cigarette.'

May could use a wee, but she didn't want to mention that.

'People come walking through woods, don't they?' said Tom. 'Workmen, and so on?'

'Woodsmen, they're called.'

'And lumberjacks.'

'Not usually in the evening, though.'

'Then we need a dog walker to come by, or a horse rider.'

But what if no-one came by? How long did it take to die of thirst? The wood was silent except for birdsong, and the birds not only sang but flitted, seeming in their freedom to be mocking May and Tom.

May said, 'Do you think Guy suspected Nancy?'

'I think he knew that she and her brother had the best motive for killing Braddon – let's put it like that.'

'I suppose Braddon kept tabs on that moquette all along. I mean, it was the start of everything for him.'

'Reckon so, May – and he had plenty of railway contacts who'd know its whereabouts.'

Tom was moving his right hand again.

'What are you doing?'

'Breaking off a piece of bark.' *Snap*. 'OK, got a sharp piece here.' By twisting his hand he was attempting to saw the rope.

'Why are you leaving the magazine?'

'Roy's right. It's a railway magazine, and it's *his* railway magazine. I was wrong to try to make it into a general interest one. It was doubly wrong, really, because I was doing it at the behest of someone else.'

'Who?'

'The proprietor.'

'Yesterday I called him from the hospital – told him my heart wasn't in it. I said keep Roy in post and bring in a couple of young railfans to liven it up a bit, but in a railway *way*. The whole railway world is in awe of Roy.'

'That boy in Halifax knew about him.'

'I rest my case. I've put it all in a memo: maximise the number-one asset: Roy.'

'That was nice of you.'

'Being nice is not in it, May.'

'Yes, it is.'

The sawing sound had stopped.

'How are you getting on down there?'

'This sharp piece of bark isn't all that sharp. Mind if I try something else?'

He seemed to be fishing in his pocket again.

'What are you after?'

'My lighter. I'm going to burn the rope, if I can sort of hold it up in the right way. If the flame touches you, yell.'

She heard the efficient, metallic flick, felt nothing, and then, '*Ow*!

The lighter unclicked. 'Try again.'

Another click, and then almost immediately the sudden sag of the rope round her wrist. May could have danced around the wood; instead, she dashed away for a wee. When she returned, Tom was looking through the darkening trees in the direction of the road, his canvas bag slung on his shoulder. 'All set?'

May led the way.

'Say, May. Just hold on a moment.' He stepped up behind her. 'You've got a piece of bark in your hair.' Then he kissed her, and she kissed him.

When they walked on it had started to rain.

'How long will it take them to get to France?'

They were heading down a lane in the direction of the

village called Fingest. Beyond the trees, shapes that might have been rain clouds or hills had begun to appear.

'They'll be at Dover by eleven-thirty or so, then it's straight onto the steamer. Crossing time about another two hours. I'd say they'll be at Calais by two at the latest. The connecting train to Paris takes about five hours. That's if they take the ordinary boat train. There's also the *Night Ferry*. That's a train that's put on a ferry.'

'I think Braddon did a poster for it.' May was thinking of the train circling the moon.

'There are lots of posters for it. Always in the spotlight is the *Night Ferry* – and a lot of cops hang around the customs, so I reckon they'll go for the ordinary boat.'

'How much notice would Price need to catch them?'

'If you were to tell him right away he'd have a fair chance. The boat train and the steamer can be intercepted. As can the train to Paris, if he has friends in the French police . . . and he's a charming sort of fellow, I think you said? Cigarette, May?'

'No, thanks, Tom. I've given up.'

'Oh, look – a phone booth.' It stood glowing beneath a street lamp.

'Once they're at Calais,' said Tom, 'I think they'll take to the road – probably hire another car under some new name. Nancy's pretty smart. I'm sure she has it all worked out, and I think it *will* work out unless you get hold of Price before about two o'clock. Or let's say one, because of all the preliminaries he'll have to go through.'

May stepped into the phone box. All the accumulated heat of the day was in that box, which had a sweet, barn-like smell. May straightened her hair in the window glass. Beyond it Tom was lighting a cigarette beneath the lamp. She picked up the handset and joggled the hook. It didn't seem to make quite the right sound, so she replaced it and stepped out of the booth.

'No luck, May?' said Tom, blowing smoke.

She shook her head.

'Didn't think you would have.'

Fingest village consisted of a church, about six houses, a barn, a pub and another phone box, all benignly overlooked by a wooded hill. The rain had taken on a steady, soothing rhythm. 'Shall *I* try the phone this time?' said Tom.

As he walked into the booth May turned away.

He emerged after a few seconds and said, 'These country phones . . .'

'It's not as if she actually *said* she killed him, is it? Not in so many words.'

'I don't believe so.'

'What she *did* say was that, whether or not she killed Braddon, she and her brother would be running away.'

'And who's to say they're really going to France? We happened to notice that book—'

'—Doesn't mean they're actually *going* there.'

'Or there's always the States, May, via Southampton. Ocean Terminal.'

They turned towards the pub. May believed they were both noticing that the telegraph wires of the village were not connected to it. Glimmerings of light came through its windows. As it turned out, there were only glimmerings of light within as well. Oil lamps illuminated a bar; wall candles illuminated small oil paintings in ornate gold-leaf frames. Most of the light came from the good log fire. A small, stooped woman appeared, beautifully dressed in Victorian blue velvet and lace, and she was pleasant but firm. 'Sit by the fire and get dry,' she said. 'I can do you steak and kidney pudding with a nice trifle, cheese and biscuits to follow. If you want a room, we have just the one upstairs. That would be for the young lady. The gentleman can sleep down here – on *that* couch.'

So she had immediately divined that May and Tom were not married.

'Of course, there would be no *charge* for the gentleman. I can give him a goose down pillow and plenty of blankets, and he can keep the fire all night. Now, what would you like to drink?' But there was no time to answer before she said, 'I have a lovely bottle of claret.'

'Might we have an aperitif?' said May, who was determined to make some intervention in the dinner plans.

'Yes, dear, you may,' and the woman waited rather tensely.

'Two small sherries, please.'

Tom frowned questioningly, then laughed, which was what he was meant to do.

'Two small *dry* sherries. We don't have the sweet.'

21

'You're not telling me he stayed downstairs all night?'

'I'm not telling you anything, Ellie Bancroft.'

'I can tell he didn't, by your smug smile.'

'It's an enigmatic smile, dear.'

'That's what you think.'

They were sitting in the garden of Derry & Toms department store in Kensington, which happened to be on the roof of the building six floors up. The gardens were bounded by a brick wall, for obvious reasons, and the general impression was not so much of being high up in Kensington as of being abroad: in Italy, for example, or at least the Italy of May's imaginings, what with the exotic planting, the tinkling fountains, the coral-coloured flamingos taking stilted steps, the sun-faded parasol above their table on the terrace of the Sun Pavilion, whose name did not seem the least bit incongruous on this balmy first Wednesday of September. The chimes of the church below floated up through the pale blue sky. Three o'clock; Ellie and May had the afternoon off work. A woozy bee floated over their plates, which were smudged with the remains of chocolate eclairs. Ellie waved it away. 'I'm glad he came up to the mark anyway.'

'How do you mean?'

'Well, being so chivalrous and everything, and going along with your plan to let Nancy get away with it.'

'I've told you we called the police first thing the next morning. Well, first thing after breakfast.'

Ellie laughed, a little too loudly for the man at the next table, who was drinking beer and reading the *Evening Standard*, early edition. Headline: THE FUHRER SPEAKS.

'What I'd like to read,' said Ellie, 'is an article headed, "The Führer Shuts Up." What did the police say again?'

That sunny morning in Fingest the phone box next to the churchyard had been rather crowded, given that both she and Tom were in it. May had called Sergeant Price's number, which was answered by another detective sergeant, name of Spencer. Price, he said, had been 'transferred to traffic control'. When May said she was calling about the murder of Rex Braddon, Spencer had said, 'Hold on, I'll get the file.' He came back on after ten minutes to say he would call them back.

The phone box had rung half an hour later when May and Tom were lying on the churchyard grass, he reading yesterday's papers, she finishing off *Cakes and Ale*. When May told Spencer the version of her story she'd agreed in advance with Tom, he didn't think they'd been slow at all in getting in touch. 'I appreciate it that you're calling now.' There had followed quite a long silence, at least down the phone line, if not in Fingest, where a tractor was dragging a jangling plough along the road.

'Is my name on the file?' May asked, partly to make sure Spencer was still on the line.

'Not that I can see . . .' May could hear him shuffling papers.
'You do have the letter predicting a forthcoming murder?'

'Yes. Someone's written "Possible connection", then put a question mark.'

'And you have the piece of moquette that came with it?'

'The piece of what?'

'The piece of material I mentioned just now?'

Further turning of pages down the line. 'The enclosure seems to have gone missing.'

Silence down the line once again, and silence in Fingest too, except for the ticking of a passing cyclist. Eventually: 'You say they've probably gone abroad?'

'Probably.'

'Well, let's see if they come back to England, shall we?'

'And you've heard nothing since?' said Ellie.

May shook her head.

'Well, I think you did the right thing. Mrs Marshall was the best teacher I ever had.'

A ladybird had landed on one of the plates. They watched it for a while.

'Red and black,' Ellie said thoughtfully.

It had been a late summer of colour. May had been buying gloriously yellow mimosas every few days recently, partly in celebration of the *Red* magazine having quite spontaneously written to her requesting further stories. Then there had been the picnic with Tom in Hyde Park, next to a bed of very purple lobelia (another reminder of 'her' moquette), during which Tom had told her he'd got funding for his new magazine. *To Read on the Train*, it would be called.

. . . And May could easily imagine the circumstances of Ellie's most unexpected encounter, in the Rose Garden on Scarborough's South Bay, with the tousle-haired man she'd liked the look of at the West Gallery. (Ellie had talked about it often enough.) Apparently some of the roses had been a very delicate cream shade, like old parchment, a result of being grown next to the sea. Recognising Ellie, the man told her he was running summer painting classes at the Grand Hotel. He'd suggested she apply for the Royal College of Art, where he was a tutor. The upshot was that Ellie had got a place on the painting course, to start in October. (It seemed things happened fast there if they spotted true talent.) Ellie had also received a scholarship reserved for northern students. 'Who'd have thought,' she had mused to May, 'that it would ever be *useful* to be from Yorkshire?'

Mrs Henderson would be chipping in to assist. She was in Paris now but corresponding regularly with Ellie. In one of her letters she had suggested that May might have a bright future at Q&B, should she decide not to pursue writing full-time. She'd had a word by phone with Mr Quarmby himself – a directing hand was needed for women's fashions. Tom had urged May to 'give it a whirl'. She hadn't yet decided, but she had been reading a good many fashion catalogues recently, entranced by the descriptions of colours, often written in French – artificial flowers for cloche hats, for example: *velours*, in *beige*, *capucine*, *amande*, *rouge*, *jaune*.

'I notice you've ditched the little case,' Ellie said, because today May had forsaken her Gladstone bag for her lizard-skin clutch bag.

'Well, I'm not carrying the moquette about.'

'What have you done with it?'

'Nothing, why?'

'Have you thought of framing it and putting it on the wall?'

'Because all our good luck came from it?' said May. 'Yes, I have.'

'I don't think you should, though. It would be sort of . . .'

'Triumphalist,' said May. 'Like asking for two *large* sherries.'

A waiter had appeared on the terrace. Ellie raised her hand for him to come over. 'Will you, or shall I?'

ACKNOWLEDGEMENTS

The following people have kindly supplied me with factually correct information, and I have tried (usually) to stick to the facts. Any departures from them are entirely my responsibility.

I am grateful to Sue Martin and Nicola Turner for advice about art education. For information about Halifax, I am grateful to Anne Wilkinson and Paul Berry. On railway matters, I'm grateful to Niall Davitt, author, and Stephen Bigg of the Bluebell Railway; on car matters, to David Cormack; on weaving matters, Bryony Renshaw, Senior Curator, Paradise Mill Silk Museum, Macclesfield. Stephen Beamon was very helpful on 1930s police procedure (or the lack of it). Julia and Michael Pruskin were illuminating about furniture of the time, as was Penny Keiner-Ross (of 'Pennies', 41a Amwell Street, Islington, London ECIR IUR) about clothes. I am also grateful to Megan Pilgrim and Tracey McCarthy for the loan of books, and to David Bownes of Twentieth Century Posters, and Emma Sewell of Wallace Sewell, moquette designers.

SEATS OF LONDON

A Field Guide to London Transport Moquette Patterns

London Transport has always wanted the best design,
be it Charles Holden's superb art deco Tube stations on
the Piccadilly Line or Harry Beck's Tube map.

And this pursuit of excellence has extended even to moquette. In the
Thirties top artists like Paul Nash and Enid Marx were commissioned
to design patterns; nowadays every line gets its own bespoke moquette.

Andrew Martin's bestselling guide, published in association with
the London Transport Museum and drawing on its definitive archive,
covers everything from the first horse bus to the latest Tube train,
and from the possible influence of Margot Fonteyn's luggage on a
Routemaster's seats to the moquette pattern most preferred by cats.

'A wittily written book', Twentieth-Century Society magazine

'A little gem of a book and, as its title suggests,
intended to be used much like a wildlife field guide',
Text, the journal of the Textile Society

'Andrew Martin has written an intriguing book that has opened
up a facet of London's transport to a wider audience and he easily
succeeds in hitting his sitting target,' *Subterranea*

£14.99